MR McCOOL

Or

The Miraculous and Inspiring
Adventures of Kingsley Tail

MR McCOOL

JONATHAN TULLOCH

EGMONT

EGMONT
We bring stories to life

Mr McCool
First published 2012
by Egmont UK Limited
239 Kensington High Street
London W8 6SA

Text copyright © 2012 Jonathan Tulloch

The moral rights of the author have been asserted

ISBN 978 1 4052 5036 8

1 3 5 7 9 10 8 6 4 2

www.egmont.co.uk

A CIP catalogue record for this title is available from
the British Library

Typeset by Avon DataSet Ltd, Bidford on Avon, Warwickshire
Printed and bound in Great Britain by the CPI Group

45452/1

EGMONT LUCKY COIN

Our story began over a century ago, when seventeen-year-old
Egmont Harald Petersen found a coin in the street.

He was on his way to buy a flyswatter, a small hand-operated
printing machine that he then set up in his tiny apartment.

The coin brought him such good luck that today Egmont has
offices in over 30 countries around the world. And that lucky
coin is still kept at the company's head offices in Denmark.

For Aidan, Joseph, Aelred, Freyja, Anselm, Madeleine, Freddie and all the polar bears.

Contents

CHAPTER 1
Prisoner

From where Willum was standing, the polar bear didn't look in very good condition. Pelt yellow and moth-eaten, a crown of flies played about its head. Lying flat in a thin scrap of shade, the animal's mighty flanks heaved, its pink tongue lolled.

'Why is it just lying there?' someone complained from the viewing platform close to Willum. 'I want to see it move.'

Willum watched the boy, who was about his age, take out a coin and hurl it down into the pen. The coin thwacked into the bear's hide, but the Arctic animal did not stir.

'Still not moving. Boring.' Losing interest, the boy left for the next enclosure.

Willum wandered over to the information board.

Meet Mr McCool, it offered. *He's a fully grown male polar bear, measuring 2.5 metres from nose to stub tail. In the wild, polar bears live in the Arctic where temperatures drop to forty below zero.* No wonder the animal was panting, Willum thought, the spring day was warm and sunny.

The Latin name Ursus Maritimus, the board explained, *means 'bear of the open ocean'. Polar bears can swim for four days without resting.* Willum looked down at the zoo enclosure's stagnant pool. The bear wouldn't even be able to swim four strokes in there. The unfairness pricked him like a hot needle.

Lord of glacier and berg, the information continued, *the great ice bear roams freely in one of the world's last wildernesses.* Once, the concrete pen must have been painted white to mimic an iceberg, but now, an ashen, lifeless grey, it was more like a corner of the moon than the North Pole. A hole led down to a damp bunker: the captive's den.

Mankind is their only enemy, the board concluded. *Polar bears, the world's largest land predator, with a sense of smell 100,000 times more powerful than that of humans, are an endangered species. Climate change means that by 2020 this beautiful, noble creature may very well be extinct.*

Feeling his mobile phone vibrate, Willum took it out from his backpack. There was a text from his auntie, telling him they'd have to be going soon, to make it to his tutor session in time. Willum sighed. He'd forgotten about today's lesson, the last one before the entrance exam tomorrow. Putting the phone back, he felt something else in the backpack, the book he'd been reading all week instead of revising. He took it out for a quick look. *A Treasury of Greek Heroes and Myths* was far more interesting than long division, or English comprehension. If only real life could be half as exciting and magical as the incidents in this book. If only Willum could do the kinds of things that the Greek heroes did. The *first* thing he'd do would be to rescue this polar bear.

'Look, it's woken up,' somebody shouted.

Stretching and yawning, the polar bear rolled on to its back.

The visitors gasped at the sheer power on display, then groaned with disappointment as the animal lay still again.

A little girl started crying. 'I wanted to see a cub, not a mangy old thing like this.'

'It's all horrible and yellow,' a boy whined, a dazzlingly white polar bear toy tucked under his arm.

A cry of disgust rose. 'There's something in there with it. Look!' People were pointing at the pen. 'Yuck, gross! Down there,' they shouted. 'A rat. It shouldn't be allowed.'

Willum saw a flash of brown fur. *Was* it a rat, or something bigger? A meerkat maybe, or a squirrel?

People were still shouting when a burst of electric static crackled on the air. 'Ladies and gentlemen,' a tannoy announced, 'boys and girls, the march of the penguins commences in five minutes. Please head to the penguin pools for games and feeding time.'

The crowd barged its way down from the viewing platform, leaving Willum alone. Resting his elbows on top of the safety barrier, he peered down at the bear. It looked so helpless, so lifeless: a prisoner without a crime. It wasn't fair. Willum felt tears scorching his eyes.

Suddenly the polar bear lifted its great shaggy head and stared back. The animal might have been captive, but its eyes were wild, and the more Willum stared into them the deeper they seemed, until he felt as though he could actually see the ice floes and snow of the bear's natural habitat. He tried to look away, but the wild eyes held him like a pair of jaws.

Rising on two legs, head swaying, the animal clawed the air as though beckoning. To his horror Willum found himself climbing the safety barrier. He couldn't stop. Desperately he tried to wrench his eyes free from the bear's. Losing his balance, his hands danced for a grip on the barrier, and then he was falling, not quickly, but gently, twirling into the enclosure like a snowflake.

When Willum came round, the first thing he realised was that he wasn't dead. He was lying in a dark place under what seemed to be a pile of foul-smelling straw. The second thing was that an argument was going on somewhere nearby.

'Please,' an anxious little voice begged. 'Don't hurt it, big fella.'

'It's *human*, innit,' a deep-throated, cockney bass rumbled in reply.

'Hey, it can't help that. We all have to be something,' the first voice countered.

'Should 'ave thought about that before it fell into me pen,' the deep cockney shot back.

Something was rummaging through the straw towards Willum. He felt a flush of warm breath on his cheek and glimpsed a broad, bristling black nose.

'What are you doing now, large lad?' the little voice worried. 'Remember the zoo rule: *Hurt a human and say goodbye*. We're already in enough trouble with you dragging it down here.'

The straw covering Willum was clawed aside and in the dim light he found himself face to face with Mr McCool. The bear's teeth glistened like trapped moonbeams. 'Been in trouble since the day they brought me to this poxy place,' he rasped.

An electric shock seemed to sear through Willum: he could understand the bear. The bear had a cockney accent. Willum's shock congealed into cold dread as Mr McCool stared at him. Another face appeared. It was the little animal he'd seen when he was up on the viewing platform.

'Don't maul it, Big Mac,' the small creature pleaded, the pools of his brown eyes glistening. He was more of a squirrel than a rat. 'There's an 'ice bear.' He gave a burst of nervous laughter. 'Get it? I said "*'ice*" bear, not "nice", what with you hailing from the frozen lands . . .' The laughter petered out.

'Big Mac, I'm begging of you, let the human be.'

'Why should I?' Mr McCool demanded, still staring at Willum, who barely dared to breathe.

'Look at it lying there, large lad,' the squirrel-like animal said. 'Terrified's not the word. Only a half-grown, a cub, a kit, a whelp, a pup. Just like you when they first brought you here. Shoot, almost cute close up. Well, not as ugly as they look through the bars of a cage.'

'You know the old saying, Kansas,' Mr McCool growled. *'The only good two-legs is a dead two-legs.'*

Kansas hopped from paw to paw. 'A human in your den! We've crossed the line now, Big Mac. Oh, Rattlesnake Annie, what we gonna do?'

Mr McCool's reply was to open his jaws and reveal more teeth.

'No, no!' Kansas cried.

As the huge, yellowy head loomed closer, terror paralysed Willum. Turning his face to the dank concrete wall, he waited for the worst. A few seconds passed. Why didn't the animal strike? Every tendon in Willum's body stretched to snapping point with the sickening suspense. Then he heard the strike of a match, followed by the smell of smoke and a racking cough. Willum looked round to see that the bear had retreated to a corner, and was smoking a cigarette.

'Say, Big Mac, thought you'd given that up,' Kansas scolded.

'Started again, ain't I?'

'I wish they'd stop throwing those firesticks into the pen. They make you cough like a prairie thunderstorm. Can't be good for you,' said Kansas.

'You tell me one fing what *is* good for me in this stinking dump,' the bear snapped. 'Now shut your mouth, Kansas; I need to fink. Got to work out what to do.'

The smoke in the den thickened and the silence tightened like a noose until Willum felt that he was being choked.

'We're breaking out,' the bear declared at last, dark eyes glinting.

'Say again, big fella?'

'We're busting out, little fella. That's what we're going to do.'

'Hey,' Kansas grinned. 'Thought I was the joker round here.'

'Ain't no joke. Never been more serious. Don't you see, little fella? This is what we've been waiting for all our lives. A human in our power.' Mr McCool's deep voice broke with excitement. 'Stone the Arctic skuas – we're always talking about escaping, ain't we? But that's all it ever was, just talk, until now. Wiv a human to help us, we really *can* escape. Go and tell the lions that the time's come for them to pay back that favour. They'll know what you mean.'

'But –'

'Just go!' Mr McCool roared. 'No time to lose.'

Almost falling over himself in shocked excitement, Kansas darted over to a little hole in the concrete and shot down it.

Sick with dread, Willum watched Mr McCool pacing the confined space of the den. Smoking his cigarette to its bitter end, the bear muttered to himself. 'Risky . . . course it's risky . . . dangerous . . . Kansas could get hurt . . . or worse . . . *Impossible* . . . impossible *not* to . . . no other choice . . . the wild . . . the wonderful, wide, free-as-the-wind wild . . . What about the human? . . . Can't do it wivout no human . . . but can't trust no two-legs . . . Going to be free at last . . . or dead . . . No other chance . . . now or never . . . all or nofing . . . bust or bingo . . . do or die . . .'

Willum closed his eyes. If he kept them shut for long enough, maybe when he opened them he'd be back on the viewing platform where people talked and animals were dumb. But when Mr McCool's monologue ended abruptly in a coughing fit Willum found that he was still a prisoner in a cockney polar bear's den.

With a punch to his own chest, the bear hawked up a gob of phlegm and spat into the straw. 'Better out than in,' he cackled. 'In more ways than one.' His sudden gasp reverberated round the den. 'We're getting out of here.'

Looking furtively over his shoulder, Mr McCool reached into a cavity in the concrete ceiling and pulled out what looked like a bone or part of an antler, attached to some kind of cord. He looked at it for a while then, taking a deep breath, strung it round his neck. 'I swear,' he whispered throatily, 'by the white pelt of the midnight sun, and the black nose of the midday night, that I ain't never going to take this off until I reach home. May the *skittery-glittery*, the dancing lights of the ancestors, guide me. May the eternal ice protect me from walruses and, for all my moons, fend off the tread of *humans*.' This last word was a snarl that gave way to a chuckle as Mr McCool spat again and reached back up into the ceiling cavity. 'Now, where's me stash. Ain't going nowhere wivout them firesticks.'

His great paw rummaged around, but he couldn't find his cigarettes. Puzzled, he shambled over to another corner and, prising away a second piece of loose concrete, stuck his head in the hole. The sound of sniffing throbbed out like a bee.

'Stone the Arctic skuas,' he growled, pulling his head free. 'Not in here neither.' With a roar of temper, Mr McCool upset drinking bowls and food troughs then padded over to where Willum lay. Seeing the backpack, he yanked it from the straw and shook it in his jaws like a dog with a rabbit. 'Where's me firesticks?' he snarled as he tossed the shredded backpack away, and with a whimper of frustration flopped on to the floor.

Frozen in fright, Willum gaped at his backpack. His *Treasury of Greek Heroes and Myths* had been ripped to pieces and thrown on to the straw. Beside it was the mobile phone.

The mobile phone.

Carefully, so as not to rustle even a single stalk of

straw, Willum reached for the phone. He couldn't quite get it. Almost silently he wriggled a little nearer. The phone was in his hand when it began to ring.

As Willum fumbled desperately to stop the sound, he felt something soft tickling the nape of his neck. A cold nose burnt his skin.

'Human tricks, is it?' the cockney bass growled right into his ear. 'Well, just try another, you little two-legged assassin, and see what 'appens.' Snatching the phone, Mr McCool tossed it high as the den roof then caught it in his jaws. He swallowed. A gurgling belch rang out, followed by a rumbling cackle.

'We've got to be ready just after closing time,' Kansas announced, bursting breathlessly into the den. 'The lions are going to create a diversion, then the beavers will . . .' He paused, his eyes whirling. 'Say, Big Mac, can this *really* be happening?'

Mr McCool reached out and gently scratched Kansas's back with the tip of a claw. 'We're leaving this evening.'

Kansas shivered with pleasure then let out a

whoop of joy. 'Shooting stars! Prairie storms! I never thought the day would come.' He raced round the den. 'Going to be free, free, free. Liberty! Fraternity! Freedomery!' He stopped abruptly. 'Say, Big Mac, what about the two-legs cub?'

The bear shook his head. 'You still don't see it, do you, Kansas? It's because of the human we're going. How else could we manage? How far do you fink we'd get wivout human help?'

Kansas jumped back. 'Whoa! We're taking him *prisoner*?'

''Ostage situation, innit?'

Willum buried himself deeper into the straw. Just a short time ago he had been looking down at a captive zoo animal. Now *he* was the prisoner. He tried to swallow but couldn't.

'By the way,' Mr McCool said. 'You ain't been throwing away me firesticks again, 'ave you?'

Kansas grinned. 'Won't be any firesticks where we're going. Won't be any humans. Won't be anything but *the wild*. Hey,' his voice trembled with awe, 'you've put the tusk on.'

The bear fingered the walrus tusk dangling from the cord round his thick neck. 'Yeah.'

'Then it *is* for real!' Yipping in fresh delight, Kansas careered about the den.

The polar bear stopped him with one of his great paws. 'Calm it, little fella. We need all our wits about us. Freedom is gonna be dangerous, tough, tricky.'

'Kind of like a rattlesnake, huh?'

'A rattlesnake and a walrus put together.'

Kansas gave a low whistle then grinned. 'Say, got a joke for you, big fella. This one'll knock you flat. A real fur-tickler.' His grin toppled into a chuckle that grew and grew until he could barely get his joke out. 'What's the difference . . . what's the difference . . . what's the difference between a walrus and an orange?'

'Dunno,' Mr McCool cackled huskily. 'What *is* the difference between a walrus and a orange?'

'Well, you'd better find out because if you ever try to peel a walrus . . .' Kansas dropped to the ground in a giggling heap.

'To peel a . . .' Mr McCool rolled over beside him just as helpless.

'To peel a . . .' Kansas cried.

'To peel a . . .' Mr McCool cried.

Kansas's laughter was airy as a spring wind

through prairie grass; Mr McCool's was as terrifying as the gusts of an Arctic gale.

'Keep 'em coming,' Mr McCool said at last. 'Gonna need all the laughs we can get. Right, time for me swim. Got to keep everything as normal, not attract attention. Humans might be stupid, but they's terrible suspicious and cunning.' The bear kicked more straw over Willum. 'This one gives you any trouble, bark, and I'll rip its tongue out.'

Deep in the straw, Willum could tell that the bear had gone outside by the sudden stirring of human voices from the viewing platform. Relief flooded through him. He flexed his limbs and took some deep breaths. The sound of a thunderous splash reverberated into the den. Mr McCool had jumped into his pool. Willum was listening to the human voices when he heard the pair of light paws digging down towards him.

'Hey, that's better.' Kansas smiled, scooping straw from Willum's face. 'Can't have you suffocating. Relax, I'm not going to hurt you. Neither's Big Mac. Just do as he says. His bark's worse than his bite . . . most of the time.' He chuckled. 'Listen to me chatting away just as if you understand every word.' Willum tried to speak but no words came. Had the shock of it all struck him dumb?

Sitting bolt upright, Kansas listened intently, counting the splashes coming from the pool. 'On his front, one, two, three, four; reach the wall, turn, flop on his back, one, two, three, four; reach the wall, back on his front, one, two, three, four . . .'

Pool circuits over, Mr McCool hauled himself from the water, shook his pelt and, just as he did every day, lumbered up the grey concrete iceberg of his enclosure. At the highest point he fell into a heavy heap. From here he could see the whole zoo spread out beneath him: his kingdom of cages. Yet today he felt no despair; this would be the last time he lay here on this ledge like a captive emperor on a concrete throne. Very soon he would be free.

Big-cat feeding time began. Mr McCool peered down across the pens to where a human throng pressed against the lion enclosure. As he always did at this point, Mr McCool hoisted himself on to his feet, and padded heavily back down to his den.

Kansas was waiting anxiously. 'We really going through with it, big fella?' he asked. Mr McCool nodded. 'Still can't hardly believe it,' Kansas whispered. 'Everybody talks about breaking out; never thought we'd actually do it.'

'The time for talking is over, little fella. Remember what I've always told you.'

'*One day of freedom is worth more than a lifetime behind bars,*' recited Kansas in a solemn voice.

Mr McCool's eyes glinted. '*One day of freedom is worth more than a lifetime behind bars.* Now all we have to do is wait.'

With Mr McCool back in the den, Willum felt his spine freeze – he wouldn't be able to run even if there was no one to stop him. Surely someone would be looking for him by now? Yet he couldn't shout to alert them. Through wisps of straw, he watched as the two animals began to play a game that resembled darts, each one throwing a sharpened object into a wooden board on the wall. The hours ticked slowly by. It was as though he had fallen not into a zoo pen but the pages of a book far stranger even than his *Treasury of Greek Heroes and Myths*. And cramped and aching on the straw, Willum couldn't have felt less like a hero.

Kansas must have slipped out of the den because

some time later Willum heard him returning.

'Room service!' the little animal declared, dragging in a small cardboard box. 'The best that the zoo bins have to offer.'

'Scoff,' said Mr McCool. Giving a grunt of pleasure, he thrust a paw into the box and snatched out a nearly full tub of Ben & Jerry's chocolate ice cream.

Willum felt Kansas's paws scurry on to the straw. He was holding out a gnawed finger of Kit Kat.

'For you,' Kansas whispered.

Kansas was eating his own piece of Kit Kat when he realised that Willum's remained untouched. 'Still in shock, huh?' he murmured to the boy. 'It'll pass. It's what predators do to their prey. All in the eye. You're maybe feeling it a bit harder than most on account of you humans having got out of the way of dealing with predators. The terror grabs hold of you so you can't move. Kind of freezes you up, pins you down. We call it *stum-sturned* or *claw in the eye*.'

As Willum stared at Kansas, a large paw swung down between them and grabbed the untouched finger of Kit Kat. 'Waste not want not,' a deep voice proclaimed. 'Now shut yer rabbit, Kansas. The human can't understand and it's getting on me nerves.'

Burying himself deeper into the straw, Willum listened to the Kit Kat disappear in one snaffling bite.

At last a lion's roar throbbed out over the zoo. Mr McCool sprang to his feet. 'Zero hour,' he growled. Closer to the den, Willum heard a gnawing sound, followed by a great creaking and tearing, as though tree roots were being ripped up. The thud that followed seemed to shake the concrete enclosure itself. 'Go, go, go!' Mr McCool barked.

Mr McCool dragged Willum from the straw, thrust him on his back and burst out of the den. The sudden brightness of daylight was dazzling.

'Geronimo!' Kansas cried, scampering up in front of Willum as Mr McCool stepped on to the oak trunk that a group of beavers had just felled. 'Gonna be the ride of our lives! Better hang on tight, human kit.'

'If it lets go, I'll snap it in two,' Mr McCool rumbled.

Clinging to Mr McCool's thick fur, Willum hardly dared look as the bear scaled the fallen tree, then, dangling over the pen wall, dropped. Landing on all fours, Mr McCool ran. As he lumbered past the other enclosures, the animals shouted encouragement, faces pressed against mesh, grille and glass. Capybaras, wild dogs, apes, pygmy hippos, camels, elephants, rhinoceroses, tapirs, zebras, lynx . . .

The runaways soon reached the service entrance's metal gate: the weakest link in the security chain. With a surprisingly skilful dab of a claw, Mr McCool unslid two bolts. The third was padlocked. He grunted and groaned, growled and gruffed, but the bolt would not budge. A shrug of his mighty shoulders sent Willum tumbling to the ground. 'Open it,' Mr McCool demanded. 'Pull back the metal tongue and open it.'

'Shoot, he can't understand you,' Kansas said, looking anxiously behind him for any sign of the zoo keepers.

Mr McCool mimed opening the gate.

'You're frightening it, big fella,' Kansas warned.

Mr McCool growled through clenched teeth. 'I'll do more than that in a minute.'

Willum staggered to the gate. There were four dials on the combination padlock. Feeling the bear's breath roasting the back of his neck, his fingers fumbled out the only combination that came to his mind: 1 0 6 6. It didn't work.

'I don't think it knows how to do it,' Kansas said.

'Got to know,' Mr McCool snarled. 'It's *human*.' He dropped a heavy paw on Willum's shoulder. 'Open it. Or so help me . . .'

With shaking fingers, Willum tried again: 1 9 6 6, no use . . . 1 2 3 4, no use . . . the day and month of his birthday, no use. He felt the paw lift from his shoulder then, through the corner of his eye, saw it whirling towards him. There was no time to dodge the talons glinting in the sun. But at the last moment the bear dropped his blow and, lowering his head, charged at the gate instead.

'Careful, large lad,' Kansas yikkered.

A crunch of bone on metal thudded out, and Mr McCool flopped to the ground. With a creak, the gate fell open. For a few seconds Mr McCool lay stunned, then, with a blood-freezing snarl, he sprang up, thrust a rigid Willum on his back and plunged across the threshold.

They had gone about ten paces when the bear realised Kansas wasn't with them. He was still by the fallen gate. 'Come on, little lad,' Mr McCool cried. Kansas didn't move. The polar bear lumbered back. 'What you doing, little fella? We can't stick around saying goodbye.'

Kansas was trembling all over. 'Can't seem to do it.'

'Eh?' said Mr McCool, his huge head leaning to one side in confusion.

'Thought of nothing else all my life, and now . . .' Kansas raised a forepaw and tried to lift it over the threshold. 'Just can't.'

'Well, I ain't going wivout you.'

Kansas smiled sadly. 'You're better off without me, large lad. Truth is, I'm growing kind of old for this lark. Oh, I know a long-lived fella like you wouldn't notice, but I'm not so spry and gladly gadfly as I once was.'

'Cobblers. Come on, they'll be on to us soon.' Mr McCool's nostrils widened in desperation.

'Rodents age quickly. Guess freedom just came too late. Now I know polar bears aren't so hot on emotional goodbyes so just go. *Git*, big fella.'

'I'm taking you wiv me,' Mr McCool fired back. 'Second 'ostage if needs be.' He grabbed Kansas, ready to throw him up alongside Willum. But his friend's gentle brown eyes stopped him.

'Freedom's got to be chosen, Big Mac, otherwise it's just another kind of zoo.'

Mr McCool's voice was small. 'What am I gonna to do wivout you?' He put the little animal down.

His whole body shaking, Kansas tried one last time to force himself over the line. 'No,' he said. 'It's not for me. Now go, Big Mac. If anyone can make it, *you* can. Do it for me. Do it for all of us. No more time to waste!'

'You was my friend,' Mr McCool managed to grunt. 'In the worst of places, the best of friends.'

Then, head down, Mr McCool ran blind. The wide world broke over him like a wave, and he stumbled. But the voice of Kansas, calling after him, seemed to lift up and steady him.

'May the eternal ice protect you,' Kansas called. 'May you blow free as the prairie wind! May you feel the snow of liberty.'

Willum heard a catch in the polar bear's breath.

'And, Big Mac,' Kansas cried. 'Don't hurt the human kit. Got a feeling that if you look after that half-grown then he'll look after you.'

CHAPTER 2
Hostage

Mr McCool shambled down the road leading from the zoo, heart banging like a breaking ice shelf. The high-rise buildings dizzied him; the foul fug of pollution bewildered him. The warm tarmac seemed to burn his paws and blunt his claws. A busy crossroads loomed ahead. Losing his nerve, he plunged down a dark alley.

Clinging numbly to Mr McCool's back, Willum found himself in a dank courtyard crammed with bulging black bin-liners, recycling banks and the stink of waste food.

Mr McCool clawed open a bin-liner and wolfed down a wad of lasagne, but he was too anxious to eat properly. Even his belch was half-hearted. He should never have left Kansas. Losing him was like losing a paw.

Just at that moment a door opened. Mr McCool's nose recognised the smell: male adult human. He lurched behind a bin, hissing into Willum's ear: 'One peep from you, and I'll shave your face off.'

The man wore a large chef's hat and a stained kitchen apron. Unsteady on his feet, he was carrying a box of empty bottles, which chimed as he tripped. 'Careful, careful,' he giggled.

Mr McCool grimaced as the man drained the dregs from each bottle then threw them into the recycling bank. The human stench was almost more than he could take. The man pulled out a packet of cigarettes and was about to light up when he caught sight of the hiding figures. Mr McCool tensed, ready to spring.

'Hello, son.' The kitchen porter winked at the boy. 'Now then, mate,' he greeted Mr McCool. A second passed then – 'Sweet Mary-Anne, it's a polar bear!' With a soft *ploff*, he fell back on to the bed of bin-liners.

Snatching the cigarettes, Mr McCool concealed them deep in his pelt and lumbered back down the alley on to the street. 'Stone the Arctic skuas,' he rumbled. 'Ain't no going back now. Do it for the little fella.' He kissed the walrus tusk then craned his neck round so that his nose was within a hair's breadth of Willum. 'Now listen here, two legs,' he rumbled. 'You cling and you cling good. Call for help or try to run, and in the name of the eternal ice I'll slash you. They might get me, but I'll get you first, all nice and filleted. Maybe you can't understand me, but you can understand *this* all right.' Resting his open jaws against Willum's face, the polar bear growled with such ferocity that, for a moment, the boy thought his bones had been shaken loose. As Mr McCool ran to the crossroads, Willum buried his face in the shaggy pelt as though in the pillow that was taking him deeper and deeper into a nightmare.

Braced for a surge of shrieking humanity, Mr McCool blundered on to the busy street and found himself amongst a large group of . . . animals. *They* were all running too. It was as though the whole zoo had escaped.

Willum squinted to read a banner hanging between lampposts: *WWF Fancy-dress Fun Run*.

'Love your outfit,' somebody in a giraffe costume called over.

'You could pass for the real thing,' a giant penguin laughed.

'Is that your dad under there, son?' a zebra quipped.

Desperate, Willum tried to shout for help. But the words wouldn't come. He was still – what had Kansas called it? – *stum-sturned*. How could any of this be happening?

Bewildered, Mr McCool joined the runners. What in the name of the midnight sun was going on? His nose wasn't deceived, these weren't real animals. Nothing could mask the human stink: that acrid cocktail of choking chemicals with which the two-legs lace their body and hair.

'I'm saving the bamboo forests,' a human panda said, coming right over. 'You running for the Arctic? Hey, nice growl, pal. Fairly set me hair on end. Those teeth of yours look real too. Just as if they could bite my head clean off.'

Years of captivity and bad habits had taken their toll, and Mr McCool's breath soon gave way. Wheezing and coughing, he stumbled from the fun runners and staggered into the watching crowd who, to his surprise, clapped and whooped. His nose told him two things: these humans meant him no harm, and water was nearby. Moving water! He recalled the autumn when the wild snow geese had landed in his pen and he'd asked them how he might make his way back to his lost homeland. *Find the flowing feather and fly home with her,* they had said. Well, he'd found the flowing feather – they'd meant running water. His spirits and nose lifting, Mr McCool followed the river's scent.

Willum held on tightly as Mr McCool trudged through the cheering crowds. Each time he decided to let go and drop to the ground, he remembered the press of those jaws and the growl that had shaken his bones. At last he felt the bear judder to a sudden halt. They had come to the top of a steep flight of steps.

Agitated by the unfamiliar obstacle, Mr McCool snarled and sniffed at the fall of steps before forcing himself to begin the descent. Faster and faster he went until he was thundering down at breakneck speed. An embankment with railings lay at the bottom. Unable to stop, Mr McCool lurched across the embankment, hit the railings and tumbled into thin air.

For a second, Willum was flying free, then he felt the shock of cold. He was in the river. Before he could sink too far, he was grabbed by the scruff of the neck and hauled to the surface. It was Mr McCool. The bear pulled Willum on to his back again and kicked downstream.

How odd this is, Willum thought to himself, fear displaced for a moment by the sheer strangeness of the situation. *When I should be at home doing sums with my tutor, here I am swimming down the river on a polar bear's back.*

A burst of deep-throated laughter broke into Willum's thoughts.

For the first time Mr McCool was enjoying the freedom of open water. 'This is the style,' he chuckled. 'This is the pukka way to go. This is . . . stone the Arctic skuas, this is flamin' knackerising.' He coughed out a lungful of river. It was one thing to do circuits in a tiny pool, another to swim in a river. Already his limbs ached, and his pelt and head weighed like boulders. With growing desperation, Mr McCool doggy-paddled for shore. He dragged himself on to a spit of shingly mud and lay there panting. They'd chanced on an old harbour, and the crumbling jetties of a dilapidated wharf rose above him. Disused barges and boats lay all around, each in various stages of decay. It was a graveyard for river craft. But Mr McCool's nose was telling him something more urgent: the two-legs was running away. He hauled himself to his feet, and saw Willum disappearing across the mud.

Sinking up to his knees in the gloop, the boy was running for his life. A wild glance over his shoulder showed him that the bear was following: a great white weight of tooth and claw gaining on him. Willum hurdled a line of old rowing boats. Tripping over the fin of an ancient keel, he jumped back up again and scuttled down a narrow gap between two rows of abandoned tugs.

Face, hands and body thick with mud, chest heaving, Willum was deep in the midst of the shipping graveyard when he turned a corner and found his way cut off by an old barge. It was in much better condition than the other craft. Frayed curtains at the window and an empty flowerbox showed that the barge had once been a houseboat. Behind, Willum could hear Mr McCool's laboured breathing getting nearer. With a desperate strength, Willum jumped on to the barge, and pulled himself up to the little engine platform at the stern. Careful not to fall, he followed the narrow ledge round the barge. It took him to the front deck where an open hatchway yawned. Catching a glimpse of white fur through the maze of boats, Willum dangled himself down through the hatch and dropped into the cobwebby hold.

'Where's it gone?' Mr McCool growled in frustration. He scented the air for the two-legs, but it was difficult to penetrate the stench of oil and rusting metal. Slipping and sliding, tongue lolling, he shambled through the labyrinth of hulks. He had to get the sneaky two-legs before he raised the alarm.

In the dusty darkness of the hold, Willum listened to Mr McCool prowling closer and closer. Over the savage drum of his own heart, he could hear the bear's increasingly angry growls. The tread of paws grew heavier, then stopped just beside the barge. Willum heard a loud sniffing. Then: 'Found you, you murderous little two-legs.'

*

Willum braced himself for the attack. But instead of a vicious growl the next thing he heard was a whimpering yelp. Mr McCool had stood on something sharp. Willum peeked over the edge of the hatch to see the polar bear dragging himself on to the houseboat's little deck, his injured forepaw held out gingerly.

Dropping back down into the hold, Willum waited, his heart thudding. Suddenly the square of light at the hatch filled with a broad, white head. But before Mr McCool could move any further there was an almighty crack: the sound of splintering wood.

'Stone the . . .' the bear swore as he felt himself falling. The rotten deck had given way. With a whoosh of dust, Mr McCool crashed into the hold.

The bear lay there without moving. His whole body ached. Since breaking out of the zoo, he'd moved more than he had done during the past ten years. More serious than that, the stabbing pain in his paw told him that he couldn't go any further for now. Nose bristling, the injured bear scented the hold. Apart from the boy's stink, the human scent was cold. No one had been here for months. This was as good a place as any to lie low until he could work out what to do next. He just had to make sure the two-legs didn't get away again.

Wedged in the furthest corner, Willum watched helplessly as the polar bear edged towards him. The great head loomed closer until the boy felt the sharp scrape of whiskers against his cheek. 'Said I'd eat you,' the bear rasped. 'Said I'd rip you like a seal.' A huge yawn prised open Mr McCool's jaws. 'And I'll do it bite by bite until . . .' Another slobbering yawn interrupted the threat. 'So if you . . .'

The bear's head fell heavily against Willum. Snoring filled the hold. Mr McCool had fallen asleep.

How soft the fur felt, how lethal the tooth resting on his neck. Pinned down by the enormous bulk, Willum crouched in the musty shadows. How could he get past the bear without waking him? And if he *did* wake him? Kansas wasn't here to intervene now. His heart bouncing like a basketball, Willum lifted the dead weight of the sleeping head, inch by inch. Any false move would be fatal.

At last, Willum managed to free himself. Now all he had to do was crawl over the comatose Mr McCool. He had almost made it when the bear let out a ripping snore, and licking his mighty chops, turned over. The whole boat shook. A flailing paw rasped at Willum's head. Ducking, Willum felt the talons pass through his hair like the teeth of a deadly comb. Mr McCool settled back into sleep.

Willum watched the light slowly fade through the broken timbers above. It was night before he risked moving again. Edging away from the bear, he hauled himself up through the hatch.

The stronger deck planks still stood, but they creaked loud as a shout as Willum picked his way over them on his hands and knees. Straightening up, he was just about to jump down and sprint away over the mud when he saw something that hit him as hard as a blow from one of those mighty paws. The boat was floating down the middle of the river.

The frayed mooring rope must have snapped under the bear's weight, leaving the barge to the mercy of the rising tide. The vessel had been sucked out of the old wharf and dragged on to open water. And, to make matters worse, a mist was gathering. Even as Willum watched from the small deck at the front of the long, narrow boat, both riverbanks were disappearing.

Without warning, a boat loomed out of the fog. As it shouldered past them, Willum tried to shout, but no words came out; he was still stum-sturned. And the fog was too thick for anybody on-board to see his frantic waving. The barge was still bobbing on the wake when Willum heard another craft heading towards them. This one sounded bigger, and closer. Willum realised the houseboat must be drifting down the wrong side of the river . . . floating *into* oncoming traffic! Frantically, he thought back to the canal holiday he'd been on last summer with his auntie. He gripped the little rail that ran the length of the barge and, stomach heaving at the thought of slipping and falling into the murky water, he groped his way round the narrow ledge to the steering platform at the back of the boat. The tiller must be here somewhere. Yes, there it was. Grasping the wooden rudder, Willum jerked it to the left to make the barge drift right. But before the narrow boat could move out of danger, the larger vessel groaned out from the mist, so close that Willum nearly choked at the stench of diesel. The wake fizzed up against the old barge, shaking it like an empty plastic bottle.

From the hold, the snores were growing agitated.

Willum sensed that there was either going to be a collision or the bear would wake.

'Come on,' he murmured, holding the tiller as far to the left as it would go. Slowly the barge edged away, but not before a third boat could be heard approaching.

Louder and louder, the oncoming engine throbbed. Then there it was, breaking from the fog. Willum felt panic tightening his throat until he could hardly breathe. It was a dredging boat, used to dig out mud from the riverbed. It had a huge metal claw that towered over the barge like a dragon's talons. With a high-pitched screech, the dredger passed. The claw had planed a huge splinter from the barge's wooden keel.

Raising one foot on to the gunwale, Willum took a deep breath to steady himself. Fog or no fog, he'd decided that his only chance was in the water. In *A Treasury of Greek Myths and Heroes* people were often swimming, and just as often – he tried to stop himself reflecting – drowning. All at once the book made sense to him. Heroics are a matter of necessity not choice. Bravery is when there's nothing else for it.

Mr McCool woke with a groan. For a few confused moments he thought he was back in the concrete bunker of his zoo den. Why was his whole body aching? Why did his paw throb like a skuas' beak? Where was Kansas? Then he remembered: he was on the run, alone and injured, a fugitive with a human hostage. But his nose told him that this wasn't quite true – the young two-legs had bolted again.

'Stone the flamin' Arctic skuas and all the bleedin' caribou too,' Mr McCool snarled. He couldn't put any weight on his paw, but he knew that he had to get out of there. The alarm would have been raised by now; any moment they'd come for him.

Mr McCool had hauled himself halfway out of the hatch when a deafening sound filled the air. Instantly he recognised the din of a helicopter; he'd often watched the two-leg contraptions buzz over his enclosure like bloated wasps. With a moan, he dropped back into the hold.

The helicopter searchlight scalded the fogbound river like lightning. 'Police marksmen are in this area,' a voice boomed through a loudhailer. 'Stay behind locked doors. A polar bear has escaped from the zoo.'

The human words whined in Mr McCool's ears like the high-pitched buzz of tundra mosquitoes, but he understood their deadly intent all too well. The hunt had begun. He kissed his tusk. *One day of freedom is worth a lifetime behind bars.* Well, he hadn't even had that long. He felt himself choke with rage. What would Kansas think when the news reached the zoo? He began to growl, softly at first, but louder and louder until he was even drowning out the police helicopter. Mr McCool wasn't just going to roll over and surrender. He'd show them how a wild animal could die. Lighting a cigarette and steeling himself against the searing pain in his paw, the polar bear lugged his wounded bulk up through the hatch.

Willum had been about to jump when the chopper had come. At last he found his voice – yet it did no good. He waved at the helicopter and shouted and screamed himself hoarse, but the rotor blades hurled his words away like snowflakes in a blizzard. Sensing movement behind him, Willum looked over his shoulder.

Cigarette in mouth, walrus tusk glinting in the

searchlight, Mr McCool rose on hind legs. Head swaying, he mauled the air as the helicopter thundered downriver. With a roar of rage, he shambled forward. He'd kill the two-legs good and proper now. What was there left to lose? 'Revenge time, innit,' he snarled.

Jump, Willum shouted silently at himself, *jump now*. But even as he tensed his body to leap he met Mr McCool's eye. Once again, he felt himself in the grip of paralysing terror, pinned down by *the claw in the eye*.

'Got you now,' Mr Cool rumbled. 'And, by the black nose of the midday night, I'm gonna finish you once and for all . . .' But even as he lifted his good paw for the fatal blow, the bear found himself hesitating. How thin the shivering boy looked, how defenceless. How much like a cub. Confused and angry with himself for dithering, Mr McCool gaped at the boy. It was now that his nose scented water on all sides. What in the name of the eternal ice was going on? He looked over the side of the barge. They were floating down the river! At that moment the barge passed beneath a bridge. There was a splash close by. Something had dropped from the parapet above. Whatever it was, it was now gasping and flailing in the heavy water.

'Help,' a little voice cried. 'Big fella, help.'

'Kansas?' Mr McCool called in disbelief. 'Is that you, little fella?'

'Sure is . . .' Kansas's words were a frothing bubble.

Willum felt the houseboat rock; a towering column of water broke over him. Mr McCool had jumped.

'Where are you?' the polar bear boomed. He swam over to his friend's gurgling voice, but found only fog. 'Kansas?' he cried, his roar ragged with urgency. There was no reply. Mr McCool thrashed lopsidedly around, his injured paw hanging uselessly. His sensitive nose could only pick up the acrid tang of the city river – and the scent of his own blood. 'Little one!' he bellowed. 'Where are you?'

Willum stood at the edge of the barge as it drifted on the current. He could no longer see Mr McCool. The bear's shouts were growing faint. In a few minutes, Willum would be free. He felt his breathing ease. Then he heard a thin spluttering in the water.

'Help! Drowning!' It was Kansas. 'Please. Help.'

Willum snatched the long boathook attached to

the top of the barge. 'Over here!' he cried. 'Grab hold.' He flailed the hook about in the water. 'Can you see it?'

No answer.

Shreds of mist swirled around the empty hook. 'Wait,' Willum shouted. 'I'll find a light.' Boathook in hand, he carefully worked his way round the side of the barge. He was crossing the deck area to the hold when his foot kicked something. Dropping to his haunches, his hands found Mr McCool's cigarettes and matches. Willum ripped the box apart, then, after a few strikes, lit a match. He fed the flame on the cardboard. He nursed the fire against the swirling fog, and held out the boathook. 'Swim towards the light and grab hold of the pole,' he shouted.

Willum felt a light touch on the boat hook. In the flare of the cardboard beacon, he could see a bedraggled Kansas clinging for dear life. Gently, Willum pulled in the boat hook and took the little creature in his arms. Both shivering in the damp chill, they stared at each other in awe.

'I can understand you,' Kansas whispered, nostrils twitching.

'And I can understand *you*,' Willum echoed.

But there was no time to dwell on the astounding revelation. 'Big Mac's still out there,' Kansas gasped. Wriggling free of Willum's arms, he scampered on to the barge roof and yikkered a series of barks. A faint roar replied. 'Please, whoever you are,' Kansas begged Willum. 'Turn this thing round and rescue my friend.'

'He'll kill me,' Willum shot back.

'He wouldn't do that.'

'He said that he'd rip me like a seal.'

'Just talking big. Hey, what did you expect from a great ice bear? Soft as anything underneath it all. *Please*, you gotta trust me.' Kansas hung his head. 'I don't blame you. Don't worry, I'll do it myself.' Tensing himself, he prepared to jump back into the river.

'Wait, you'll drown!' the boy cried.

Willum struck match after match as he searched the cupboards. The hold had been the houseboat's living room and kitchen all rolled into one, and it was still strewn with the former occupants' possessions. From the deck above, Willum could hear Kansas's increasingly forlorn yips. There was no answering roar from the bear now. Discovering an old oil lamp, Willum lit it. The flush of light showed him what he was looking for: a key hanging on a nail in exactly the same place as it had been on the holiday barge. 'Found it!' he shouted up to Kansas. That summer with his auntie, Willum had done most of the actual sailing, and he was confident he could master this boat too. But would such a dilapidated barge work? And what if he *did* save the bear?

'Hurry, please hurry,' Kansas begged. 'Save him and he'll sure change his mind about you.'

Rounding the narrow ledge to the steering platform, Willum found the engine and slid the key into the ignition. He turned it. The motor gave a dry moan. He tried again. This time, a splutter and shudder was followed by a gust of belching smoke: the engine throbbed into life. Willum felt icy sweat beading his brow. He would just have to trust Kansas. Slowly, the boat began to reverse upstream.

'That's it!' Kansas cried. 'We're going backwards.'

The noise of the bear hunt pulsed all around them. Police sirens scolded a bridge downriver; the helicopter buzzed over the city. The lantern shone forlornly on the barge roof. Although he continued to shout for his friend, even Kansas, an optimist by nature, was beginning to give up hope. Then a great gasp tore through the air and a broad head broke the fog. Mr McCool was doggy-paddling his wounded body towards them.

'Tumultuous tumbleweed!' Kansas shrieked, his little whiskered snout trembling with ecstasy. 'Spiralling sidewinders!'

Huge chest heaving, back legs kicking, the polar bear dragged himself back onboard.

'Careful, large lad, you'll have us under,' Kansas warned as the narrow boat rocked and rolled.

Coughing and choking, Mr McCool fell heavily into the barge.

'*Ice* to see you, Big Mac,' Kansas quipped, then fell down beside the gasping bear in a helpless heap of relieved laughter.

When the bear had recovered his breath, his nose lifted and located Willum at the back of the barge, on the steering platform where the engine was still throbbing. 'Get the two-legs to turn that racket off and then bring it here,' Mr McCool told Kansas.

'Hey, Big Mac,' Kansas said. 'The two-legs saved you.'

'Just fetch the human, little fella.'

Kansas scurried over the barge's roof to Willum. 'Come with me and don't speak,' he whispered when Willum had turned the engine off. Willum hesitated. 'What's the matter?' Kansas asked. 'I'm telling you, the large lad is going to thank you. Once you get to know him, you'll see that butter really wouldn't melt in his mouth. Anyway, no use trying to make a run for it – the big fella's nose could find a corncob on a prairie.'

Breath ragged, Willum followed Kansas.

'Take the hostage down below,' Mr McCool commanded.

'Shoot, large lad, if it hadn't been for the human, you'd still be –'

'It was just a trick,' the bear growled. 'To catch us.'

Kansas shook his head. 'You're getting it all wrong; we should be thanking it.'

Willum peered at Mr McCool. He didn't seem very grateful. And it wouldn't only be butter that would melt in those glowering jaws.

'What you looking at?' Mr McCool demanded. Then he gave a roar of rage. He'd found his cigarettes lying soaked on the deck. 'Did you do that?' he demanded of Willum.

'It was me, big fella,' Kansas said quickly. 'Just an accident, when I was scrambling. Hey, time for a joke.' Kansas chuckled anxiously. 'You're going to love this one. It'll crack you up. Cracked me up. What do you get if you cross a polar bear with a seal?' He could barely stifle his giggles. 'You get a . . . you get a . . . you get a polar bear. Get it? See, if you leave a polar bear and a seal together, then the polar bear will eat . . .'

But Mr McCool wasn't laughing. And when Kansas saw the way the bear was glowering at the young two-legs his laughter fizzled out too.

'Don't hurt him, Big Mac,' he whispered. 'That kit saved our lives.'

'When you gonna learn, little fella?' Mr McCool snapped. 'There ain't no good going around on two-legs.' He turned back to Willum. 'Maybe I'll let it off for now,' he muttered, eyes narrowed to slits, 'but see the next time it tries to dob me in? I'll eat it. So help me, I'll start wiv the lips then gouge out the eyes, and for me main course, the heart and liver.' Nudging the relevant part of Willum's body with his nose, Mr McCool emphasised each course of his meal.

'You don't mean it, large lad,' Kansas protested uncertainly.

Willum felt a wave of sickness.

The bear growled even more threateningly, but the growl became a whimper when he banged his injured paw against the deck.

'Hey,' said Kansas. 'That doesn't sound too clever. What's happened?'

'Noffink,' Mr McCool snapped. But as he tried to hide his injury, something glinted in the lantern light. A sharp piece of glass was embedded between his claws.

Suddenly Mr McCool scooped up Kansas in his good paw, and hugged him. 'Thought I'd lost you forever, little fella,' he said in a voice choked with emotion. 'Thought I was gonna have to do it wivout you. Why'd you change your mind?'

'Got to thinking you might want a few jokes on your journey,' Kansas said. 'Not to mention a spot of light excavating.' He lifted his forepaws and pulled the foolish grin that always made the bear roar with laughter. 'Got to thinking one day of freedom really *is* worth a lifetime behind bars. Got to thinking you're the best friend I've ever had. That was enough to get me over the line. Then it was just a matter of the rodent grapevine. Bunch of rats told me you'd been seen on the river. They led me through the sewers to the bridge you went under. Some smell.' Kansas grimaced. 'Still, the gutter gang seem to like it.'

'You could 'ave drowned,' rasped the bear.

'Worth the risk,' Kansas replied, a shy smile on his face. 'And here we are.'

Mr McCool smiled back. 'Here we are.'

'Are we free, big fella?'

'We're free, little fella.'

'Free. Didn't know a word could taste so good.'

Both animals breathed in deeply then exhaled solemnly. Willum watched the bear through the corner of his eye. Kansas had been wrong; Mr McCool still hated him.

'Let's do one,' the bear said. 'Got to get out of sight. Them humans is on the prowl, big time. And this one we've got here is as slithery as one of your rattlesnakes, and tricky as a walrus. It tried to trick me by luring me to this floating den, but looks like our luck's in. This is just what we need. Remember what the snow geese said about *flying the feather of water home?* Well, we're flying it, little fella, flying it nice and high.' Mr McCool yawned. 'Knackerising business, this escaping malarkey. Fink I'll get me some shut-eye.'

CHAPTER 3
All at Sea

The barge drifted downstream, bear snores rattling the hold. Willum lay in the darkness, expecting to collide with a bridge or another boat any moment.

'You awake?' Kansas whispered.

'Yes,' Willum whispered back. He felt Kansas scamper up his arm.

'Can I ask you a question, human kit?'

Willum nodded.

'Who are you?'

Morning would soon be breaking behind the frayed curtains at the portholes, and Willum could just make out the warm pools of the little creature's eyes. 'I was going to ask you the same thing,' he said.

'Well, you first,' urged Kansas.

Willum thought about the question for a while then shrugged. 'I'm Willum.'

'Never heard of a Willum before.'

'No, that's my name. I'm . . . well, I suppose I'm a human.'

'The regular type of human?' There was wonder in Kansas's tone.

'I think so.' Willum could hardly believe his next words: 'What about you? You're a squirrel, aren't you?'

Kansas gave a soft chuckle. 'Right kith, wrong kin. A *kind* of squirrel, but not of the tree flavour. Second guess.'

'Some kind of meerkat?'

Kansas laughed so heartily that Mr McCool whimpered and licked his lips in his sleep. When Kansas spoke again it was in an even lower whisper. 'I'm a prairie dog, and I've got a great joke for you. You'll love it. What do you call fifty penguins standing at the North Pole?' He held his head in his paws to try and smother yet more giggles. Willum glanced anxiously at the dark mass of Mr McCool. 'Lost!' Kansas spluttered, then doubled over with laughter. Willum could feel the creature's warm fur tickling his cheek. 'Listen, Willum,' Kansas whispered into his ear. 'If I was you, I'd sling my hook whilst his lordship's asleep. I won't wake him. Seems to me one favour deserves another.'

'Thank you – Kansas,' Willum said.

'Thank *you* – Willum. I know you're still just a kit, and I hate to think of your parents worrying about you.'

Fumbling through the gloom, Willum was making for the hatch when a low *psst* made him stop dead. He turned.

'Will you tell the others to go easy?' Kansas asked.

'Others?'

'The human race. Tell them to stop the war.'

'What war?'

'The battle against paw, beak and claw. I hear tell you're not going to give up until there's none of us other animals left in the wild.'

A picture of the zoo with its concrete, stagnant water and coin-throwing visitors popped into Willum's head. He nodded slowly. 'I'll try,' he replied.

As he climbed back up on deck, dawn was breaking. The fog had lifted on a beautiful morning. Perfect for a little swim. Soon *he* would be free. But as Willum's eyes adjusted to the bright light of the new day he saw that there was just one problem. The fingers of the rising sun were holding a vast horizon of water. During the night, the houseboat had drifted out to sea.

Willum sat on the barge roof gazing at the receding coastline. Any chance of escape was gone. Not only that: how long could an old riverboat stay afloat on the open sea? Fortunately it was calm. From below, Mr McCool's whimpers were becoming more and more pronounced until at last the animal woke with a howl. Willum listened to Kansas trying to soothe his grumbling friend. How glad he felt that Kansas was with them again.

A scurry of light paws brought Kansas up on deck. 'Hey, Willum,' he said. 'I thought you'd –' Then he noticed the sea. The prairie dog scrambled up on to the roof beside Willum and peered at the water in wonder. 'A prairie of water,' he breathed. After a time, Kansas's gaze returned to the barge with its worn wood, splintered deck and faded paint. 'Your den a good floater, Willum?'

A pained roar rose from below. 'He's got a heart of

gold, you know,' Kansas whispered. 'Deep down. He'll come round. Just talks tough. Put it this way, he can't be that bad, otherwise *I'd* have been a bite-sized bear treat long ago.' The prairie dog sat up and pulled one of his funny faces. Willum smiled. 'Seems you've got yourself caught up in our mess, Willum, so I'd better explain one or two things. For a start, probably better we *don't* let on you can talk. Not until he's got to know you. You'll have picked up by now that his lordship's none too fond of humans. Got his reasons, believe me: suffered pretty badly at your hands; snatched from the ice when he was little more than a cub and brought to the zoo. Real sob story, upsets me just to think of it. Imagine how you'd feel without a mum or dad.'

'I don't need to,' Willum replied.

'Why not?'

'My mum and dad are both dead.'

Kansas's eyes pooled. 'Hey, I'm sorry.'

'It was a plane crash.'

'What's a plane crash?'

'Oh, it all happened a long time ago. I'm used to it. In fact, I don't usually tell anyone.'

'Well, I'm glad you did,' Kansas said. 'It may not

be much consolation but as from now you got yourself a new friend.' Scuttling up Willum's arm, the prairie dog rubbed noses with him. Despite the situation, Willum found himself laughing. 'That's better, Willum. We're all going to get on famously, you'll see. I knew it the moment I first saw you.'

A cry rang out from the hold. 'The big fella's not doing so swell,' Kansas explained. 'Paw's pretty tender. Got something stuck in it. Say, don't suppose you could help him?'

'Like Androcles,' Willum said.

'Huh?'

'He was a boy who pulled a thorn from a lion's paw.'

'Aha! Could you get hold of this Androcles to come and help?'

Willum laughed again, and shook his head. 'He's from Ancient Greece.'

'Where's that?'

'Nowhere – not any more. Well, he's just in a book I've been reading.'

'A book?' Confusion muddied Kansas's eyes.

'It's a story,' Willum explained.

Kansas puffed out his cheeks in surprise. 'Humans have stories too?'

Willum nodded.

'Hey, do you think *you* could do it, Willum? Do an Androcles with a polar bear?'

'I could try.'

'That's the spirit.' Kansas skittered over to the hatch, but paused before going down into the hold. 'By the way,' he murmured. 'What happened to Androcles in the story?'

'The lion became his friend.'

'I knew it! What are we waiting for? Time for you two to become friends. Come on.'

Taking a deep breath, Willum followed Kansas down into the hold. Sprawled over an old sofa, Mr McCool was moaning softly to himself. On catching Willum's scent, he lifted his head suspiciously.

'Say, Big Mac, it's going to look at your paw,' Kansas said, gesturing for the boy to go nearer.

Mr McCool growled. 'Noffink the matter wiv me paw. Them firesticks dried out yet? Gasping for a smoke.'

'I've seen your paw, large lad. Nasty. You need help.'

Willum looked at the injury. The pad round the

shard of glass was swollen and angry-looking. The bear's small ears were limp.

'All right, but any tricks and I'll claw its eyes out,' Mr McCool growled. He scented Willum in confusion. The bear could detect no threat from the human; neither could he register any malice. Mr McCool decided to be doubly careful. No matter what Kansas said, the last thing you should ever do is trust a two-legs.

'The human will have to pull it out,' Kansas declared. 'Might hurt some.'

'Pain don't bother me,' the bear snarled back, taking the walrus tusk between his teeth.

With the morning sun streaming through the threadbare curtains, Willum reached out and took Mr McCool's paw. It weighed heavy as a rock; power coursed through the spread of claws like high voltage in a cable. Willum's mouth ran dry. Taking a deep breath to steady his hand, he gripped the piece of glass. Maybe they *would* be like Androcles and the lion. As he began to pull, all at once he felt calm . . . and the large shard slipped easily free.

'Nice job,' Kansas cried. He gave a low whistle.

'Big as one of your teeth, large lad.' He hopped over to lick the wound clean.

'What you gawping at?' Mr McCool growled at Willum.

'Hey, don't snarl at Androcles, big fella,' Kansas grinned.

'*What?*'

'You'll be right as ice in no time, large lad. *Snow* pun intended.'

'Right,' Mr McCool declared. 'Now that that's sorted it's time for . . .' His nose gravitated towards the kitchen area like the needle of a compass. '*Nosh,*' he cackled, then hobbled over on three paws to the cupboards and smashed a door in. He pulled out a giant packet of prawn crackers, ripped it apart and guzzled the contents, except for a single cracker he threw to Kansas.

'What about the human, Big Mac?' Kansas chuckled.

The bear spoke with a full mouth. 'What about it?'

'Willum needs to eat as well.'

'*Willum?*' Mr McCool growled.

'I mean humans,' Kansas said hurriedly.

Mr McCool clawed down a drum of marshmallows.

Piercing the plastic with a claw, he tossed Kansas and Willum one each then, with a jerk of his head, swallowed the rest. A stinging belch followed. 'Passable,' he pronounced.

'Distinctly passable,' Kansas added, the pouches of his little cheeks bulging with stale marshmallow. 'But the human's going to need more than just that. Look at it, big as an ostrich.'

With a begrudging grunt, Mr McCool coughed up a few marshmallows and spat them at Willum before rummaging deeper in the cupboard. Willum wiped the gunge from his cheek. The lion hadn't behaved like this to Androcles.

'Say, what you got now, Big Mac?' Kansas asked.

'Dunno,' the bear replied. Gnawing open a bag, his tongue dived into the kilo of sugar. There was an appreciative rumble. 'This is a bit of all right, little fella.'

'Sure is,' giggled Kansas, dipping his head into the bag.

Willum watched Mr McCool demolish a box of dates, then a huge tin of hot chocolate, and after that a packet of spaghetti.

'Rattlesnake Annie, it's raining food,' Kansas cried

as the bear threw over a few tit-bits.

Seeing the others eat made Willum feel hungry. His last meal had been yesterday lunchtime. The spaghetti was no good but, to his surprise, the dates were lovely. Then he dipped his finger into the hot-chocolate powder – it was delicious. He felt a touch on his shoulder and saw that Kansas had run up there and, with his soft tongue, had begun cleaning the chocolaty smears from his chin.

With the houseboat's out-of-date food supplies demolished, Mr McCool rolled out a two-litre plastic bottle from one of the cupboards.

'What's this then?' he mused. It dropped to the ground and rolled away. With a growl, the bear retrieved it and chewed the neck off. There was an explosion of sticky, fizzy pop in his face. When the froth had subsided, he licked away the brown liquid beading his fur and the pool seeping into the floor.

'Not bad,' he said. 'There's another one in there. Get the human to open it. You seem to be able to make it understand.'

Kansas mimed opening another bottle. Carefully Willum unscrewed the cap from the second bottle of Dandelion and Burdock. He filled a pan for Mr

McCool, and a saucer for Kansas. Then, as the other two lapped theirs, he lifted the bottle to his own lips. He hadn't realised how thirsty he was. Pop had never tasted so good.

A deafening bear belch rang out. 'Not half bad at all,' Mr McCool announced. He yawned. 'Had food and drink, now want sleep. Siesta time, innit. Kansas, you guard the hostage. If he tries any tricks, just bark and I'll . . .' Flopping on to a sofa, Mr McCool was soon fast asleep.

'Who'd have thought the world could be so wide?' Kansas said, sitting on the barge roof beside Willum. The coast had disappeared. The gentle heave of the sea made the barge's frail timbers creak. 'Funny not to be looking through bars,' Kansas went on. A great tearing snore reverberated from the hold. The prairie dog nodded. 'That's all the big critters ever did back in the zoo: eat some, sleep some; eat some more, sleep some more. We little fellas could come and go, duck and dive, slip through bars and bury under wires, but your lions and bears had to do the time straight. At least the lions had company. Big Mac was all alone. Imagine that, year after year.'

'He's free now,' Willum said, to cheer Kansas up.

'Yeah, free,' Kansas grinned. 'Yes, siree. Destination, *The Wild*. Bound for the eternal snows. We're taking the big fella home. Back to the white fur of the midnight sun; back to the black nose of the midday night; back to . . .' Kansas stared deep into the horizon as though he could already see the North Pole. When he glanced back at Willum his eyes were misty. 'And it's *you* we've got to thank, Androcles. All of this – because of you. And Big Mac *will* thank you; I know he will. Right. So how we going to get there?'

'What do you mean?'

'What do I mean? Nice gag!' Kansas laughed uproariously. 'Hey, you *do* know the way to the eternal snows, don't you?'

Willum narrowed his eyes as he too stared into the horizon. 'I suppose it's north.'

'North?'

'That way.' Willum pointed over the sea. 'The sun rises in the east. So that's north. That's the way.'

'Attaboy! You can work the rest out as we go along. Between you and me, I reckon it might take us a bit longer than Big Mac thinks. The wild snow geese told him they do it in a moon. Slower by water than air though. But you seem pretty good at making these floating dens work. Now would you look at that! Ain't they a sight?'

A line of gulls was flying past the barge.

'Now then, fellas,' Kansas greeted them. 'Nice day for it. We in the right direction for the top of the world?' The gulls replied with loud, mocking shrieks. 'Mnn,' the prairie dog considered. 'Maybe all wild animals aren't so pallsy-wallsy.'

One of the gulls turned round and headed for them. A huge bird, its wingspan was almost the size of Willum.

'That's more like it,' Kansas said. 'Come for a chat, have you?'

The words froze on his bewhiskered snout as the vulture-like gull swooped. Willum flared his arms, and with a voracious squawk the gull flapped away.

Willum picked up the trembling prairie dog. 'Cross between a rattlesnake and a walrus, that's what the large lad said *the wild* would be like,' Kansas whispered. 'Didn't mention anything about wings.'

As they watched the gulls slip from view, Willum noticed that the sea was growing choppy. A wave broke at the boat's hull sending up a spray of spindrift.

Kansas licked the drops from his snout. 'Salty,' he grimaced. Another wave broke. 'Salty *and* cold,' he shuddered, shaking off the water from his coat. The waves grew until the barge was rocking from side to side. 'Should it be doing this, Willum?'

'I don't think so,' Willum replied.

Higher and higher the waves mounted, sending the pair scrambling off the roof on to the splintered little deck. The boat rocked violently and a deep groaning came from its bowels. Willum felt a punch of fear to his stomach. Was the barge breaking up? Then he saw Mr McCool's head thrust itself through the hatchway with a great moan.

'Make it stop,' Mr McCool demanded.

'We're not doing anything,' Kansas returned.

'You *must* be! Why else is it shaking?' Mr McCool cried. 'Everything's sloshing about inside me. Me belly's like a snowflake in a blizzard. Make. It. Stop!'

'It's not us, Big Mac,' said Kansas.

'I'm dying,' the polar bear cried.

With a shuddering roar, he tumbled back into the hold just as a curtain of water broke over the barge. Kansas was knocked head over heels, and slammed against the gunwale. Willum was thumped to the deck too, his breath snatched away. As the water seethed through the scuppers, the torrent sucked Kansas towards the open sea. Just in time Willum plucked him to safety.

'Shoot,' Kansas said, spluttering out brine. 'Am I glad we're friends.'

Willum struggled back to his feet. A huge metal ship had just sailed past. The sea all around was thick with vessels: oil tankers, chemical tankers, bulk carriers, container ships and ferries. The barge had strayed on to a busy shipping lane. Willum rounded the ledge to the steering platform at the back of the boat, Kansas clinging to his shoulder. Already his feet were growing used to the barge's narrow spaces. Starting the engine, he grabbed the tiller. But there was no time: they were heading straight into the path of an oil tanker. It rose above them like a rusting glacier.

'Look out!' Kansas cried. But there was nothing they could do. The barge was being pulled into the huge vessel's tow like a stick to the edge of a waterfall. A scream of smashing timber, and they were hauled across the steel hull. The tanker's engines became a din.

Kansas took a last look at the great, blue prairie of the sky. 'One day of freedom,' he whispered.

Some time later, Mr McCool's head emerged from the hold. The sea was calm; he no longer felt ill. 'Ain't dead, Kansas,' he called. No reply. His eyes widened when he saw that the front of the narrow boat had lifted right out of the water, whilst the stern had plunged beneath like a dabbling duck. 'Stone the Arctic skuas,' he rumbled.

The sea was strewn with flotsam and jetsam: oil drums, polystyrene wedges, plastic bails, plastic bottles, wooden palettes, tyres. But there was no sign of Kansas or the boy. Mr McCool roared in frustration. A *human* trick. He should have seen it coming. He'd dropped his guard for a second and now look – the two-legs had done off with his friend.

'Where are you, little fella?' Mr McCool cried. He lifted his head as high as he could and sniffed the air, but he found only the salt scent of the water and the human pollution from the floating wreckage. With a groan of its rotten timbers, the barge sank a little further. Unbalanced by the sudden movement, the bear rolled into the sea.

Clinging to an oil drum, Mr McCool kicked his way though the debris. 'Kansas,' he shouted at the top of his voice. 'Little fella?' Where was his friend in all this salt water? Dread weighed him down like a stone. He thrashed faster and faster. He was beginning to panic when he caught the faint scent of prairie dog and human. 'Bless the eternal ice!' he growled, following his nose.

At last, Kansas came into view. Adrift on a wooden palette, he was standing on the human's head waving his T-shirt as a distress flag.

'Hurrah!' he yelled. 'Hurrah for Mr McCool.' Jumping down from Willum, Kansas danced a jig on the palette, sending out little patterned ripples over the sea. 'Big Mac's OK too! The large lad lives to eat another day.'

Willum watched the polar bear kick his way over. Pelt thinned by the water, his teeth and claws appeared sharper. And he'd thought he'd been out of danger when they'd somehow managed to escape the oil tanker.

'Big Mac,' Kansas cried. 'I thought you'd . . .' The prairie dog stopped, choked with emotion. 'The human's saved me three times now.'

Mr McCool grinned at his friend, but didn't even look at Willum.

'There were metal whales,' Kansas explained breathlessly.

'Metal whales?' the bear replied.

'They came from nowhere, big fella. Almost pulled us down. If it hadn't been for Willum –'

'For *who*?' Mr McCool growled.

Kansas grinned foolishly. 'I mean for the human.'

'You called it Willum. *Again*.'

Kansas paused only for a second. 'Rodent slang. A *Willum* is a young two-legs. *Will-um*, one sound for each leg. But I gotta tell you what happened. We were dragged down right along the metal whale and if the human hadn't kept hold of me, I'd have been lost.'

But Mr McCool wasn't listening. His nose had led him to a shrink-wrapped plastic bail floating nearby. He swam over and clawed it open to reveal hundreds of family-sized wine-gum boxes. 'Black ones is nicest,' he decided, after bolting down two boxes. With a cackle, he tossed a box over to Kansas. 'I fink you might approve, little fella.'

Willum opened the box for the prairie dog and handed him a couple of sweets. 'De-licious,' Kansas whistled. 'The black ones are *definitely* the best.' Willum's mouth watered. Wine gums were his favourite sweets. 'Hey, you eat some too, Willum,' Kansas whispered under Mr McCool's loud chomping. 'I can tell you want to.'

As Willum chewed gratefully, the taste took him back to his usual life: school, the internet, a tube of wine gums after tea. Yet here he was, clinging to an oil drum in the middle of the sea, along with a polar bear and prairie dog. And there was nothing he could do about it.

At least green ones are still the best, he thought.

'Shoot, they're *all* nice,' Kansas laughed. 'Rattlesnake Annie, who'd have guessed they laid on food like this in *the wild*?'

All three hung on to the oil drum and kicked their way back through the flotsam and jetsam to the barge. Only its prow was clear of the water now. 'Doesn't look too good,' Kansas commented.

'Get the two-legs to sort it,' Mr McCool said. 'That's what he's here for.'

At the beginning of the barge holiday with his auntie, the owner had shown Willum how to use the pump should any water get into the craft. If he remembered rightly, the pump room was at the very stern of the barge and would already be well under water. How could he get there without his extra weight making the barge sink? As it was, it looked as though the boat might go down at any second. The thought of being caught in the bowels of the barge as it sank flashed through Willum's head. What worse nightmare could be imagined? Yet what other choice was there? For the second time in short succession, Willum realised that bravery and necessity are the same things.

Willum lowered himself through the hatchway. The hold was half full of water. Negotiating the floating settee, he waded to the open door that led down into the submerged passage. The pump must be at the bottom of the passage. Would it still be working? Would he remember how to operate it? There was only one way to find out. Willum took a deep breath and dived.

Hands fumbling, he groped his way down the passage, gripping what must be a row of bunk beds. He felt curiously detached, as though he were watching himself in a film or going through the motions of some computer game. But the water was real enough and Willum's breath was giving out by the time he located the pump. Turning, he hurried back.

'Did you manage, Will?' Kansas grinned from the floating settee as Willum reappeared.

Willum shook his head, then took an even deeper breath than before, and dived again. He hauled himself back past the bunks to the pump. Calmly as he could, he recalled every detail from the demonstration on the holiday. The basic principle was simple: the pump sucked up the water and expelled it through a hose.

Air bubbles streamed out of Willum's nose and up his face as he switched on the pump engine. The vibrations told him it was working. Snatching the hose, he wrestled it back up the passage, but already he'd been underwater too long. His chest felt as though it were going to explode as he fumbled past the bunks, and the pressure squeezed his head like a nutcracker. Lungs screaming, he butted forward expecting to reach the air. But he found only more water. He began to panic. Again and again he thrust out his head in vain. In his confusion had he doubled back on himself? Was he still down at the stern; or was the narrow boat diving like a submarine?

Just when he'd given up hope, Willum found his head breaking into the hold. Choking and spluttering he clung to the settee and retched up the water he had swallowed.

The hose thrashed about like a snake as it spewed out seawater. Catching the nozzle, Kansas leapt up through the hatch. The pump expelled gallon upon gallon, sending great arcs out over the sea, dowsing Mr McCool who had doggy paddled over to a crate of crisps. 'Hey, what's the idea?' he demanded.

'Rattlesnake Annie! He's rescuing us,' Kansas shouted.

The barge was already beginning to lift.

'*He?*' Mr McCool demanded.

'I meant, *it*. It's rescued us,' Kansas laughed. 'The Willum's rescued us!'

'Big deal,' the bear grumbled. 'Anyone could have done it.'

After recovering his breath Willum climbed shakily back up on deck.

'Here's the hero,' Kansas cried, licking his face. 'Our champion. Hey, and here's a joke to celebrate.

You'll love it. What do you call a polar bear caught in the rain? You call him . . . you call him . . .' Holding his sides as his laughter bubbled over, the little prairie dog rolled across the deck. 'You call him a drizzly bear.'

Willum too found himself grinning and then laughing out loud. He'd never been called a hero before. He knew he wasn't one, yet he could barely believe what he'd just done. Is this how the Greek heroes felt: as though they'd grown another ten centimetres?

But Mr McCool wasn't celebrating. Having wolfed down several kilos of floating chocolate oranges, he swam back, pushed Willum aside and tumbled down into the hold. 'Stone the Arctic skuas,' he complained, collapsing on to the sofa. 'Me back's playing up somefing rotten. Get the human to clean up.'

The bear was soon snoring. Willum and Kansas found a bucket and mop and cleared up around him. They carried out all the seaweed and brack left behind by the water, and were nearly finished when a great rumble sounded out. A few seconds later, Willum heard it again.

'It's coming from the big fella's tummy,' said Kansas.

A third rumble woke Mr McCool himself. 'What's the matter wiv me?' he cried, small ears flattened in alarm. 'I'm grumbling like a walrus's backside.'

Kansas placed his ear against the bear's growling stomach. 'What you got in there, large lad?'

'Noffink.' The bear's head craned suspiciously on its thick neck, as he considered his stomach from every angle. '*That's* the problem,' he declared. 'Ain't eaten hardly noffink since breaking out – noffink proper. And me belly's getting angry.' A claw gingerly prodded the belly; it growled. 'See?'

Kansas's eyes widened in awe. 'Big Mac, I think you must be *hun-gery*.'

'What you on about, little fella?'

'Your belly's empty and wants to be filled. You want food, but don't have any.'

'Want food? Too right I do. Sick of all this sweet rubbish an' all. Want proper grub. Like what I used to have.' Mr McCool placed his paws on his belly and whispered dreamily: 'Cod heads, halibut gizzards, salmon fillets, the works.'

'And does sir require a bucket, an enclosure and a concrete paddling pool to go with that?' Kansas began to laugh.

'What's funny?' Mr McCool demanded over his growling belly.

'Don't you see, large lad?'

'No I flamin' well don't.'

'You're *hun-gery*. The ones on the other side of the bars always used to talk about it. Rats, mice, moles, the fox. Mouth dry, throat thick, belly hollow and angry –'

'*That's* how I feel,' Mr McCool moaned.

'And that's what the wild ones call being *hun-gery*.' Kansas nodded. 'Now we're *hun-gery* too, we really *must* be free.'

Mr McCool's voice was low. 'I don't like being *hungery*.'

'Then you'll have to find some food, big fella. Hunt, forage – that's what they do in *the wild*. When there's no one to *give* it to you, you've got to find your own food.'

'Why's it always me?' With a self-pitying grunt, the bear heaved himself off the sofa and laboured up through the hatch. But there was no more floating food, and he soon came back. 'Little fella, I can't stand it. I've *got* to eat.'

'Try to sleep, big fella,' Kansas coaxed. 'When you wake up, maybe there'll be more floating food.'

But Mr McCool couldn't sleep. 'If this is freedom,' he suddenly shouted, 'then you can shove it where the snow never lies!' He savaged a corner of the sofa, chewing some of the foam before spitting it out in disgust.

'All right, all right, Big Mac,' Kansas said in alarm. 'I'd been holding these in reserve.' He produced two boxes of wine gums. Mr McCool swallowed them, cardboard and all, then threw himself on to the sofa and settled back to sleep.

Kansas gestured for Willum to come up on to the barge roof with him. 'Think we'd better stay up here tonight, Willum. The large lad's in a funny mood; bit like a bear with a sore head, I guess.' His grin wasn't as sure as usual. 'He sure is getting *hun-gery*. I hope we find some food soon.'

Willum nodded. The idea of being adrift at sea with a polar bear was one thing, but a *hungry* polar bear . . .

'Say, I bet you're *hun-gery* too,' Kansas said. 'These

are for you.' He handed Willum two wine gums. 'Shoot,' he said, watching Willum eat. 'Did anyone ever tell you how much you humans are like the orang-utans? It's in the hands; the way you reach.' Chuckling, Kansas chewed his own sweet. 'Know what he means, though, the big fella. You could get sick of the sweetness.' He held up the uneaten half of his wine gum. 'Feels like a wasp grub, but tastes sort of like honey. Only not as clean.' The prairie dog's nose wrinkled. 'There'll be some more floating food tomorrow, won't there, Willum? There'll be something for the big fella to eat, huh?'

'Yes,' said Willum, only wanting to cheer Kansas up.

As they sat there, the sun began sinking. It was Willum's second evening on the barge. A ship's funnel passed on the horizon, too far to hail. Slowly, Willum's shadow lengthened over the narrow boat. When he began to grow cold, the prairie dog sidled closer, his warm coat sharing its heat. *I must stay awake*, Willum urged himself miserably, listening to the bear's restless snores. *I must stay awake.*

CHAPTER 9
Castaway

His empty stomach growling like a savage walrus, Mr McCool peered at the sleeping two-legs. Just one nip to the neck, and it'd be meat. Enough to fill six buckets, maybe more. Saliva flowed from the bear's jaws. He'd never known torture like this before. Being *hun-gery* was like a madness, but it could all be smoothed away with a few hearty bites. He opened his mouth and prepared to kill. Yet, despite the terrible raging urge of his appetite, he couldn't bring himself to do it. After a lifetime of bitterness and hatred, now that it was possible he was unable to take his revenge.

Worse, the great ice bear felt pity for the boy lying on the barge roof; pity for a *human*. How could he explain it? Might Kansas be right? The little fella liked this human. Mr McCool looked down at his friend sleeping snuggled against the enemy. Well, it was true, the two-legs *had* seemed to help them. *Seemed*. But what did any of that matter? He was a two-legs; he and his kind were guilty. Besides, his stomach was emptier than a viewing platform after closing time.

Gently nosing Kansas to one side, Mr McCool opened his mouth, closed his eyes and set himself to rip Willum's throat out. But even as he leant down, Kansas's words echoed in his bewildered mind: *Just like you when they first brought you here*. Mr McCool closed his mouth and opened his eyes. The young two-legs had woken and was staring at him.

In horror, Willum watched the bear's head loom towards him. There could be no mistaking the famished animal's intention. With a shout, he kicked out with all his might. His foot hit the bear on his only weak spot: flush on the nose. Mr McCool fell back in shock and pain. But he was in for a far greater surprise.

'If you eat me, you'll never get home!' Willum burst out as loud as he could.

Mr McCool almost rolled off the barge in astonishment.

'Yes, I *can* talk,' Willum shouted.

Head swaying in utter bewilderment, Mr McCool's black nose worked furiously.

On a surge of adrenalin, Willum confronted the bear. Mr McCool backed away. 'It's a long, long way to the eternal snows, and without me you don't have a chance of getting there.'

'Say, what's all the commotion?' Kansas demanded sleepily. His brown eyes instantly took in the situation. 'Oho.'

'And I can help you get more food,' Willum continued breathlessly. 'You'll starve without me.'

'The kid's right, Big Mac,' Kansas put in.

The polar bear gaped at Willum. 'What, in the name of the midnight sun, are you?'

'Same as us I guess,' Kansas laughed anxiously. 'A mammal on a floating log.'

But Mr McCool wasn't listening. Nose travelling up and down the boy, his roar of frustration fluttered Willum's hair like a storm gust. 'Can't work you out, two-legs.'

'Say, Big Mac,' Kansas offered. 'No need to glower at him like that. The boy's not going to bite your head off.' A burst of nervous laughter. 'I said the *boy's* not going to bite *your* head off, but you're the one –'

The polar bear darted forward, sending the barge bobbing. Willum lost his footing and fell. For a moment it seemed that Mr McCool was going to rip out his throat after all. But instead the bear slunk past, and looking like someone who has just seen a ghost, took himself back down into the hold.

'Didn't I tell you he liked you?' Kansas chuckled. 'Course it's no wonder he's a tad untrusting of humans. I mean it wasn't only the way they cub-napped him. There's what they did to his mum as well. Now *that* really is a sad story. Just thinking about it gives me the blues.' The moonlight surprised a tear in Kansas's eye. 'Shoot, breaking my own rule. Each day has enough sorrow without carrying yesterday's with you. That's why I keep the jokes coming. Well, I'd better go and see how he is.'

Hands still shaking, Willum stood alone on the barge roof. Mr McCool could easily have finished him off, but he hadn't. The same thing had happened on the river. Why? Kansas kept telling him that the bear's bark was worse than his bite. Deep down, even after a lifetime of captivity and cruelty, did

Mr McCool really have a heart of gold?

From the hold came Kansas's gentle tone as he tried to soothe his friend. Soon the bear was snoring.

Not daring to close his eyes, Willum watched the night slowly pass, and the dawn break. He stood up and stretched his cramped limbs.

'Ahoy, bargees,' a strident voice suddenly called out.

Willum looked over the bow to an empty sea.

'Other side, nincompoop.'

He swung round and saw that a raft had come alongside the barge. Cleverly constructed from wooden pallets and oil drums, it even had a little deckhouse made with driftwood. *Nothing will ever surprise me again*, Willum thought as a very large ginger tabby cat emerged from the deckhouse and sprang on to the barge. He wore a red woollen mariner's hat, and standing on his hind legs, his deep green eyes looked directly into Willum's.

'Chop, chop, boy, one's luggage isn't going to make its own way on-board.' The cat indicated his raft. 'Not exactly one of the beautiful pea green sisterhood, but needs must.' He shuddered at the pair of makeshift oars lying beached over the raft. 'Imagine *me*, Kingsley Tail, renowned throughout the seven seas, having to *row*. Look at my paws, worn to shreds. It's an outrage. I'm an artist, a genius, not some kind of galley slave. Well, go to it, dunderhead, get my stuff.'

In his amazement, Willum obeyed and dropped down on to the cat's dinghy. The deckhouse was a well-appointed little area, with cushions and rugs. Seeing a sailor's chest, he set to pulling it out.

'Careful, dobbin,' Kingsley commanded from the barge above, long tail fluttering like an amber rainbow. 'Objects both valuable and fragile within. Oh, I'll do it. You bring the soft furnishings. And make sure you don't drop them in the water.'

Though it was heavy, the cat snatched up his trunk and sprang back on to the barge. Willum clambered after him with the rugs and cushions.

'Count them then,' Kingsley ordered. 'The rings on my tail. I can see you admiring them.' Willum stared in wonder at the marmalade tail, which was hooped with paler, honey-coloured rings. 'Well, how many, O doltish one? Count them on your fingers.'

Not knowing what else to do, Willum held up both hands with fingers and thumbs lifted.

'*Ten*,' the cat scoffed. 'And the rest. Can't carry, can't count – what *can* you do? I've never been so insulted in my life. *Ten*.' Kingsley flourished his tail so that the rings shone in the watery sun like pale gold. 'Speechless, eh? Naturally, it's the finest appendage on both sides of the Azores. As I told you, the name's Kingsley, emphasis on the first syllable. *King*sley Tail. Now summon your master. I take it that even such a sorry junket as this wouldn't have *you* in charge.'

'Howdy,' Kansas said, appearing from the hold in which Mr McCool was still sleeping fitfully.

'A rat, how charming. First of all one finds a floating garden shed; now here's the vermin to go with it.'

'Hey, I'm a prairie dog.'

'That's your story, you stick to it; to the rest of us, however, you're clearly a rodent.'

'Shoot, rodents have feelings too,' Kansas said, pulling one of his faces.

The cat did not laugh. 'An interesting theory.'

'Want to hear a joke, friend?'

'Pity me, a rat with a sense of humour.'

'You'll like this one,' continued Kansas, undeterred. Why did the –'

'I sincerely hope you're not like this all the time,' Kingsley interrupted.

Willum watched the cat's eyes narrow, his tail thicken and his whiskers comb the air suspiciously.

'There's a dog on-board, isn't there?' Kingsley hissed. 'And I don't mean one of the stub-tailed rodent variety. I need hardly tell you that graceful felines such as I do not mix with canine hoi polloi.'

Kansas chuckled. 'There's no dog.'

'Then what's that excruciating dander on the air?' Kingsley demanded. 'If I'm not mistaken, which I never am, there's a large and coarse-haired omnivore on-board this creaking, leaking bucket, and it's got canine teeth and bad breath.'

'Cross my heart and hope to die, I'm the only dog on-board,' Kansas returned.

The cat bowed graciously. 'All right, animal honour, I trust you; thousands wouldn't. Now, about the sleeping arrangements: I must have my own cabin. Unlike your ilk, cats do not rove in packs. And I'm not sharing with that human simpleton. Bring my luggage.' The marmalade tabby sprang down into the hold. A second later he sprang back. 'Why didn't you warn me about the sealhead?' he demanded.

'Sealhead?' Kansas returned.

'The goon in white, the snow gorilla, that savage killer lying on a couch in your hold?'

'Oh, it's just Mr McCool,' Kansas said, looking at Willum.

Willum nodded.

'Oh, it's just Mr McCool,' the cat returned with a mocking nod. 'The famous daisy-chain maker.'

'He's an honest, good-natured fellow,' Kansas said. 'Deep down. I mean, when he gets to trust you.'

Kingsley shook his head and dropped his voice. 'That coarse-haired carnivore makes a rottweiler look fey.'

'I've known him all my life,' Kansas responded. 'He's a softy.'

'A softy, eh?' The cat looked craftily at Willum. 'I see the two-legs isn't so certain.'

A large, broad head appeared in the hatchway, its black nose twitching. 'Who are you?' Mr McCool demanded.

Kingsley tensed, ready to spring back on to his raft at any moment. This situation would require all his expertise. 'Who are *you*?' he shot back.

'Polar Bear,' Mr McCool conceded.

'You don't say. Well, as I've told your rodent here, I'm a –'

'Moggy,' the bear finished for him.

Kingsley's tail wagged at the bear like a finger. 'Actually, I don't care for that term.'

'There was often a moggy hanging around the enclosures,' Kansas grinned.

'Didn't you hear me say that I consider that term offensive, rat boy?' Kingsley enquired coldly.

'What you up to, prowling about?' Mr McCool growled.

'Firstly, I'm not *up* to anything. Secondly, I don't *prowl*. Thirdly, I resent the fact that you're treating me like some kind of stowaway. The only creatures likely to stow away on this piece of driftwood are woodlice. I'm a castaway; it's your duty to take me. I also happen to be the finest fish chef on the high seas. My food is simply the best.'

Mr McCool's nose wobbled. 'Food, hey?'

'Yes, food,' Kingsley confirmed. 'A simple word that even our less educated brethren tend to understand.'

'*Want* food.'

'I beg your pardon?'

'Want food *now*, Moggy.'

Kansas grinned. 'Big Mac's used to large portions.'

'Yes well, *Big Mac* can wait. It isn't lunchtime. Neither could you call it elevenses.'

'Don't care what you call it,' blurted Mr McCool. 'Want nosh now.'

'I'm not in the habit of operating a snack bar.' Kingsley's tail combed the air like a radar. Underneath his bluster, the bear didn't *seem* much of a threat. His paw was injured too. The rodent was a low-class type, but harmless enough. The cat's tail quivered at Willum. 'And just how does Simple Simon fit in here?' he demanded.

Despite the insult, Willum had to stop himself from grinning.

'Willum saved us three times!' Kansas grinned.

'He's helping us out,' Mr McCool put in evasively.

The cat had made his decision: it would be easy to establish his authority over these three no-tail misfits, or his name wasn't Kingsley Tail.

'My kitchen's down here, I take it,' he declared, springing into the hold. His head reappeared in the hatchway a few moments later. 'Oven inadequate, pans pathetic, utensils from the sabre-toothed tiger epoch. All this one can accommodate, however the complete lack of comestibles renders my situation insurmountable.'

'Come again?' Mr McCool demanded.

'When he looked there, the cupboard was bare,' Kingsley said.

'Hey, nice gag,' laughed Kansas. 'The cupboard's *bare* because a *bear* –'

'I get the picture,' Kingsley interrupted. 'This just gets better and better. One has to provide the food as well.' Taking a key from under his hat, the cat opened his sailor's chest. Screening the contents from the others, he extracted a bamboo pole.

'A fishing rod,' Willum said.

The cat's emerald eyes widened. 'He can talk. The plot thickens. Although with you three no-tails it couldn't get much thicker.'

Kansas hopped from paw to paw. 'Gonna catch us some fish?'

With a final, searching look at Willum, Kingsley sprang on to the roof. 'Rather I knitted you a woollen waistcoat, rat boy? Now, polar bear, if you want some lovely, juicy fish to eat, then take my chest below and be careful with it. There's a good oik.'

Tail fluttering bumptiously, Kingsley cast his line. In no time, he was reeling in a large fish. The sound of purring filled the air. Mr McCool reached out for the catch.

'What on earth do you think you're doing?' the cat demanded.

'This,' said the bear, bolting down the fish. 'Sweet.'

'Now look here,' Kingsley snapped. 'If you're going to do that, I simply won't catch another fish. So back off, bulk boy. Do you understand?'

Nose puckering, Mr McCool grunted.

'I'll take that as a yes,' Kingsley decided.

Soon there was a pile of fresh fish on the roof.

'Right, let's get this show on the road,' Kingsley declared. 'You, boy – the talking two-legs – you're my assistant. I'd thank the others to stay out of my way. The air's already a little odour-loaded down there.' He glanced craftily at the bear. Yes, things were going to be all right here. Big, smelly and ugly as he might be, a cat could handle this Big Mac character. Just let him taste Kingsley Tail's fish of the day and he'd be in his thrall forever. 'You shall be summoned when required, O unfragrant ones,' Kingsley announced.

Willum found himself smiling at the pompous cat as he followed him into the hold.

'Get me some firewood,' Kingsley began.

Before long, the stove was roaring and the scrumptious savour of frying fish percolated the barge as Kingsley sang happily to himself.

'Knock that vacuous grin off your face, Simple Simon,' the cat commanded, 'and lay the table.'

Trying hard to stop laughing, Willum brought out some chipped plates and tin mugs from one of the cupboards. He used a tea chest as a table.

Kingsley shuddered. 'One wasn't expecting silver service, but this place has all the atmosphere of a litter tray. At the very least let's have some light. Clean the portholes, boy. Here's some soap and hot water.'

With skill and panache, Kingsley flipped the fish, adding a soupçon of herbs from his personal store. Just because he was forced to slum it didn't mean he had to lower his standards. The hold was spartan, but it had potential. Now that the grime was being removed from the windows, it was already lighter. He'd soon add a touch of style. Naturally the barge would need to be overhauled, it was scarcely seaworthy, yet it was better than where he'd just come from. Kingsley's tail drooped at the memory of his last ship, where he'd been little more than a slave. Self-pity washed over him. What had he done to deserve this life, forever castaway among strangers? When was the last time anyone had ever stroked or treated him like a pet?

As it always did, the smell of his own genius dispelled the cat's melancholy. 'Perfection,' he pronounced. Clapping his paws together, he turned to Willum. 'Go and summon Rodent Robert and the Arctic chav.'

'Dishing up?' Mr McCool demanded, head appearing in the hatchway as he inhaled the rich aroma of frying fish.

'If you mean that the meal is ready, then yes.'

Kingsley had commandeered a deckchair for himself, and sat at the table in its deep curve, legs crossed daintily. Willum crouched on a low stool, Kansas perched on the tea chest beside him. Still standing, Mr McCool emptied his plate in seconds. 'Want more,' he grunted.

'I want, never gets,' Kingsley shot back, tail quivering with annoyance.

Shambling over to the kitchen area, Mr McCool hoovered up the fish tails, scales and guts, then gave a towering belch.

'Really,' the cat cried. 'The manners of a dog.'

Willum watched Mr McCool uncertainly. How would he react to the overbearing newcomer? Dipping his head into the frying pan, the bear licked up the fish oil and grease.

'Hey, Kingsley,' Kansas smiled, chewing happily. 'This sure is tasty.'

'Of course it is,' the cat replied.

'Yup,' Kansas added. 'Real tasty.'

'You've already said that,' Kingsley informed him. 'Kindly enlarge your vocabulary.'

Having exhausted the edible possibilities, Mr McCool was now rifling through Kingsley's chest.

'Excuse me,' the cat called over. 'No thank you.'

'Nosh,' the bear moaned. '*Hun-gery.*'

'No, you're stupid and greedy. There's a difference. It takes time for one's stomach to get the message that it's full; especially in your case, given the yawning disparity between brain and stomach size. Just relax and pay homage to the culinary masterpiece.'

The insult appeared to have no effect. Mr McCool

couldn't pay attention to anything except filling his stomach. 'Want more. Couple of minnows might be all right for a moggy, but a great ice bear needs somefing proper.'

'Proper?'

'You heard me, Tabby.'

'Don't call me tabby, you ignorant, bob-tailed, soon-to-be-extinct shagpile hearthrug.'

Kingsley knew he'd gone too far. He lowered his tail and his legs and braced. If the sealhead attacked, he could spring over him and out of the galley.

'Time for a joke,' Kansas put in uneasily. 'It's a real cracker. What's a cat's favourite colour?' Despite the tension, his body bucked with laughter. *'Purr . . . ple.* Do you get it? As my old grandpappy used to say, the old ones are the best.'

'Two things, Rodent Robert,' Kingsley returned, holding his nerve even as Mr McCool's nose jabbed at his whiskers. 'Firstly, I'm here to tell you and your grandpappy that that's possibly the feeblest joke I've ever wasted time listening to. Secondly, cat jokes are not acceptable.'

'And I'm here to tell you to catch more fish,' Mr McCool ordered. 'A lot more. Now!'

Kingsley nodded. Just now discretion was the better part of valour. It was clear that the bear wasn't a serious threat. He could easily be controlled by food.

The line of Kingsley's fishing rod whistled through the air. He caught fish after fish. Mr McCool devoured them as quickly as Kingsley could reel them in. 'If I'd wanted to do this with my life, I'd have opened a fast-food joint,' Kingsley muttered.

'Full,' Mr McCool declared at last. Bissfully unsteady after his heavy feed, he lurched down into the hold to collapse on the sofa.

'In a moment I'm going to wake up and all this will be just a bad dream,' said Kingsley. He closed and then opened his eyes theatrically. 'Alas, no. Still marooned amongst the bargees.' Heavy snores rattled out. Kingsley sighed. 'Just my luck – a couch potato with teeth.' He turned to Willum and Kansas. 'Now the sealhead is out for the count, it's time for some straight answers. Just exactly who are you?'

Kansas shrugged. 'My name's Kansas, the big fella down there is Mr McCool and this is Willum, or Androcles.'

'Cut the comedy names, Mr Rentokill,' the cat

interrupted, 'and tell me what you're doing out at sea together.'

'We're a team, Kingsley.' Kansas grinned at Willum. 'A team of three. We can be a team of four, if you like.'

'Cats don't do teams.'

'You could learn.'

Kingsley shook his head pityingly. 'Call yourself a team? A *losing* team maybe. I give this floating litter tray two, three days at the most. The moment a wind blows she'll sink. If we don't reach land soon and undertake some emergency repairs, it's goodbye chums.' His tail fluttered in Kansas's and Willum's faces. 'Something doesn't ring true here. Do you really expect me to believe that a voracious polar bear would team up with a rat and an intellectually challenged child?'

'Me and the large lad escaped from the zoo,' Kansas explained.

'Zoo animals,' drawled Kingsley. 'Well, that explains it. But how does the two-legs come into it?'

'He's our friend,' Kansas replied. 'He helped break us out.'

Kingsley's green eyes interrogated Willum.

'I saw them at the zoo,' Willum said, a picture of the enclosure coming into his mind. 'And I thought, this isn't fair, they should be free. And then . . .'

'Hmm,' the cat murmured suspiciously. 'Presuming at least part of your story is true, then where are you going?'

'We're following the snow geese,' Kansas replied.

'Hardly precision coordinates, rat boy. Specify actual destination.'

Kansas chuckled. 'We're headed for the great icelands at the top of the world.'

'The North Pole,' Willum explained. 'We're taking Mr McCool home.'

Kingsley burst into laughter. 'Now that *is* a good joke. Rodent Robert, the pug-tailed polar plebian and Simple Simon the pie man sailing to the Arctic in a glorified garden shed. Any of you ever been to the frozen north? Thought not. Well, let me tell you I was once in Baffin Bay where the whale fish blow, and the ice there would crush this crate into kindling. Just as well I've turned up to save you from yourselves. Right, take me to my quarters. I require a generously proportioned cabin somewhere insulated from the shagpile's snoring and smell.'

'How about a bunk bed,' Kansas offered. 'One of them's not as wet as the others.'

But the cat wasn't listening. His eyes narrowed as they stared at the horizon. The others gazed in the same direction. After a while Willum thought he could make out a line of grey rocks.

'Amateurs' luck,' Kingsley pronounced. 'Dunderheads United have scored. Land ahoy!'

CHAPTER 5
Island Sanctuary?

'I'll repeat this once and once only. I'm *not* going to swim,' Kingsley declared as he dropped anchor. 'Unlike you coarse-grained oafs, we cats have delicate fur, sensitive to salt water. And I can't take this garden shed any nearer to the shore without splintering its hull.'

'How else you going to get there, then?' Mr McCool demanded, gesturing across the little bay to where an island rose from the sea, rocky and grey. A thin drizzle had begun to fall.

'You, my moth-eaten shagpile carpet, shall double as our rowing boat. Put it this way, if you want any more fishy foody-woody then you'd better oblige.'

Muttering darkly to himself, Mr McCool was soon

bobbing in the sea. The cat climbed down on to his back.

'Mind me ears,' the boat growled.

Holding Kansas in his arms, Willum carefully lowered himself on to Mr McCool's back. With Kingsley around, he felt safer.

'Full steam ahead,' Kingsley declared. 'The hearthrug ferry. Keep steady, oaf, I'm carrying priceless tools.'

'If you pull on that walrus tusk again, I'll roll you in the drink, moggy.'

The drizzle thickened; a curtain of grey cloud drew itself over the island.

'A real premier tourist destination,' Kingsley remarked. 'I *don't* think so.'

In contrast to the murky air, the water was clear as glass. A fathom below, Willum could see kelp waving in the current and sea urchins shining like gems. A crab scuttled between rocks. Looking up to share the beauty, he met Kansas's grin.

'Shoot, now ain't that pretty, Willum? Like something from the zoo aquarium – but swimming free.'

They soon reached the rocky beach. The rest of the island was shrouded in low cloud. Just a few scattered birch trees and clumps of bracken could be seen rising into a mizzling mist.

Kingsley sprang on to the shore. 'First of all we need wood. Go to, dunderheads. I'm going to repair your floating cattle trough, but even miracles require raw materials.'

Mr McCool shook his dripping pelt.

'Careful, you clumsy clot,' Kingsley snapped, dodging the shower.

With a smirk, Mr McCool lifted his head to scent the air. 'That nose is one of the marvels of the animal kingdom,' Kansas whispered. 'He'll be able to smell any danger.'

'I'm surprised it can smell anything over the abrasive musk of polar pleb,' Kingsley retorted.

'Coast's clear,' Mr McCool pronounced. 'Definitely no humans. Except . . .' He glanced at Willum.

Willum met the bear's eye for a moment then looked away. He hadn't felt the usual claw of terror.

'Right, as I was saying,' Kingsley began. 'Hearthrug, you –'

'Let's get this clear, Tabby,' Mr McCool growled. 'I don't take orders, especially not from no alley tom cat.'

'How dare you?' Kinglsey spat. 'I happen to be a very rare breed –'

'You're a moggy.'

'Well, since you take that tone, shagpile, there's something *you* ought to hear. Without *my* assistance, not only will you starve, but you'll get about as near to the Arctic as one of the stones on this island. You *need* me. Your good fortune resides in the fact that not only am I an expert chef but also there's precious little I don't know about shipwrighting. Ships and dishes: just two of my many talents.' Kingsley's long tail flourished high, its bristling tip darting provocatively in Mr McCool's face.

'Many talents, huh?' Kansas asked. 'Say, do you do impressions as well?'

Without moving his mouth, Kingsley said: '*Shoot, do you want to hear a joke?*'

It was the perfect imitation of Kansas.

'Wow!' the prairie dog grinned.

'*Still hun-gery,*' Kingsley rasped in a deep gravel voice. It sounded as if Mr McCool really was speaking. '*Want more fish.*'

Kansas rolled over in laughter. 'Stupendous! Say, can you do Willum?'

'I don't do humans,' Kansas returned loftily. 'They're stupid enough as it is without further parody.' He clapped his paws. 'Enough of this marvelling over my talents. Go to, ill-assorted no-tails, gather as much wood as you can carry. My challenge is to transform this fat-bottomed canal lubber into something approaching an ocean-going clipper.'

The drizzle was lifting. Kansas scampered after Mr McCool, who was lumbering down the rocky beach. 'Hold on, Big Mac. Wait for the rest of the team.'

'Firstly, I ain't part of no team wiv no two-legs,' Mr McCool snapped over his shoulder. 'Secondly, he's a 'ostage so don't go making friends wiv him.'

'You don't mean that, large lad. I can see you've already started to like him.'

'Like him?' The bear shook his head. *Like* him? He's human.'

'Like him or not,' Kansas returned, 'we need him, Big Mac.'

'Not for much longer,' Mr McCool retorted, shambling away.

Kansas waited for Willum to catch up. 'Notice anything?' he grinned. 'Big Mac's started calling you *he*. Trust me, you'll be best buddies before you can say Rattlesnake Annie. You *do* trust me?'

Willum reached down and stroked the prairie dog. 'Yes,' he said. 'I trust you.' Together they watched Mr McCool trudging down the beach. 'How did they capture him in the first place?' Willum asked.

The rodent shook his head. 'Told you, Androcles – each day has enough sadness of its own without borrowing it from the past.

'Did he have any brothers or sisters?'

'He arrived at the zoo half grown and all alone, a bit like you.'

'He must have been lonely.'

Kansas's little snout quivered. 'The story goes that he howled and fought the bars for the whole of his first moon. Shoot, who can blame him? To go from the great Arctic forever to that prison.'

'What did they do to his mum?' Willum asked. 'You said that –'

Kansas interrupted with a shake of his head. 'Maybe he'll tell you himself one day.'

They'd soon gathered a great pile of driftwood:

pallets, crates, lobster pots, wooden spars, branches and even a whole tree trunk.

'The genius is ready to commence,' Kingsley announced. He threw some sacks at Mr McCool. 'Go inland and gather supplies. Collect whatever you find that's edible.'

'Seems to have forgotten that *he's* edible,' Mr McCool muttered to himself, loping into the fog. The rough, mist-covered ground rose steeply beneath his scrambling paws and he was soon out of breath, but he felt a welling excitement. His heart was lifting inside him like a rising sun; his nose had begun to dance. Mr McCool had picked up a scent of which he had dreamt for years: a broad expanse of empty land. Suddenly he stumbled free of the fog. He had reached the top of the hill. There, below, stretching from his paws for as far as the nose could see, was a glen, purple with heather.

'Not a metal bar, piece of mesh nor wire; not a paying visitor in sight,' Kansas whispered, coming up behind his friend. 'Just the good earth in no hurry to meet the sky. Say hello to *the wild*, big fella.'

Willum arrived at the crest of the hill to find Kansas and Mr McCool awestruck on the threshold of freedom. His gaze travelled over the panorama too.

'Head's spinning,' Kansas murmured. 'The whole world too; everything's spinning under my feet.'

'Dizzy,' Mr McCool mumbled. 'Why's the ground moving?'

Kansas peered worriedly at Willum. 'What's happening?'

'Sounds like vertigo,' Willum said. 'People get it when they're standing on top of a cliff or a high building.'

'Well, it feels like we're perched right on top of the world here,' giggled Kansas. 'Maybe we've got freedom vertigo.'

'I feel it too,' said Willum. 'A bit. I mean, I've always lived in the city. This is the most beautiful place I've ever seen.'

Yelping like a cub, Mr McCool suddenly tumbled down through the heather. With a yipping cry of delight, Kansas followed, nosing through the little purple flowers. Willum too threw himself into soft heather, shouting for joy.

They'd been playing for a while, roly-polying faster and faster down the hillside then running back up to the top, when Mr McCool felt his pelt tickle. His scratching made the itching worse. He tumbled over and over, but the irritating prickling grew stronger. He looked down at himself; his yellowy-white fur was covered in tiny flies. 'Stone the Arctic skuas,' he moaned, 'I'm being eaten alive.'

Kansas had also begun scratching at the tiny flies on his body, Willum too.

'Midges,' the boy said seeing the clouds of tiny insects.

'Midges everywhere!' cried Kansas. 'And, wow, are they *hun-gery*.'

Mr McCool sprinted across the heather at full tilt, but like smoke rising from the heather, the midges swarmed after him. Finding a clump of bracken, Willum plucked a large frond and placed it on his head. The piece of fern stayed in place like a three-cornered hat.

'What's that for, Androcles?' Kansas asked, back paw scratching his fur desperately.

'Helps keep the midges away,' Willum replied, placing a small frond of bracken on Kansas's head.

'Shoot,' Kansas grinned. 'It works! Not perfect, but at least it gives you some relief. Come on, let's tell the big fella.' Kansas looked over at Mr McCool and burst into laughter. The big bear was immersed to his nose in a pool made by a mountain stream tumbling over rocks. 'Would you look at that? The big fella's having a nice cold bath.' The polar bear was singing a deep-throated song and spinning his tusk happily. 'You wouldn't get very far,' Kansas whispered to Willum, who'd been staring out over the mile upon mile of heather. 'That's if you're still thinking about going. The large lad's nose can scent a human halfway across a prairie. Besides, seems a pity to bolt just when you and him are becoming friends.'

'But he hates me,' Willum said, looking doubtfully at the great ice bear gargling under the little falls.

Kansas chuckled. 'Believe me, he likes you, just can't admit it yet. The prejudice runs deep. Give him time. The best burrows aren't dug in a day. Shoot, if you still want to go, I'll help as soon as there's a chance. Now would you look at that,' he said, pointing to a clump of heavily laden apple trees. 'Have you ever seen the like?'

'It's an orchard,' Willum said, following Kansas. A ripe fruit thudded to the ground. 'I didn't know apples could be *this* big,' Willum said in amazement.

'Or this tasty,' scrunched Kansas. 'So jaw-full, so chaw-full, so plenty-full, so belly-full. Sure beats anything they used to lay on for the ring-tailed lemurs.'

Another apple dropped, big as a melon. Willum picked it up and bit into the succulent fruit.

'Tasty?' Kansas beamed.

'Kindly enlarge your vocabulary,' laughed Willum, imitating Kingsley.

Catching the scent of the rich, russet fruit, Mr McCool hauled himself out of the water. 'Nosh?' he asked.

'Elevenses,' Kansas replied, cheeks pouched with apple as he too imitated the new member of the crew.

Mr McCool hoovered up the rest of the windfalls then, raising himself on his hind legs, he clawed at the overhanging branches. The ripe fruit drummed to the ground.

'Who's the two-legs now?' Kansas grinned. 'Paw seems to be healing nicely. Well done, Willum.' The bear continued to gobble apples. 'Say, large lad, aren't we supposed to be *collecting* supplies?'

A contented belch: Mr McCool was full. They filled

the sacks and carried them back to Kingsley, who was drawing up plans. The fog had lifted from the coast too. Further down the shore, beyond the rocks, the great arc of a white beach could be seen racing itself to sea. With loud whoops, Mr McCool and Kansas sprinted on to the sands.

'Oh, the joys of the escaped convict,' Kingsley remarked to Willum. 'But do you really think our zoo-two have the slightest chance of getting to the North Pole?' Without waiting for a reply, the cat held out a piece of paper. 'Can you read as well?'

'I think so,' replied Willum, only just managing to hide his grin.

'It's my list of requirements, dunderbread man.'

'Heather,' Willum read, starting at the top of the list.

'For storing the apples,' Kingsley nodded without looking up from his plan.

'Crabs, winkles, mussels,' Willum continued.

'Basically, gather all manner of shell fish.'

'Quantities of seaweed.'

'My kelp soup is a gastronomic sensation. Now go to – you and the other chavs are disturbing my concentration.'

*

Using a tiddler net they'd found in the barge, Kansas and Willum began fishing the rock pools.

'Hey, Big Mac,' Kansas called to the bear. 'Come and have a go at this.'

'No fanks,' Mr McCool replied coldly. 'Someone's got to go and get the heather.'

When Mr McCool came back, the others were still fishing, laughing and joking. He sat on a boulder glaring at them.

'Want to hear another one?' Kansas asked Willum, who nodded. 'I'm on a seafood diet. I see food and I eat it.'

'Jealous?' Kingsley asked Mr McCool.

'Nah,' Mr McCool lied. *'Hun-gery.'* He prodded his stomach. There was a rumble. 'When's nosh up?'

Kingsley chopped up some of the kelp that the others had gathered. He added a crab, a sprinkling of his own secret ingredient and then cooked it over a driftwood fire.

Mr McCool drained his bowl the moment it was placed in front of him, then he wolfed the leftovers straight from the pot.

'Haute cuisine on an industrial scale,' Kingsley

remarked, shuddering. 'Now, off you go. I need more wood.'

The tide had gone out, leaving the barge balanced between rocks, allowing Kingsley to work on the hull. By late afternoon the vessel was barely recognisable as the old flat-bottomed, shallow-drafted barge. Kingsley had strengthened and widened it, and added a keel. As evening fell, the others helped him dismantle the roof and replace it with a shining deck. Then, on Kingsley's orders, Mr McCool hoisted a tree trunk into place.

'Behold a mast,' the cat declared. 'Shoot, he's a genius,' he went on, imitating Kansas. Then, 'How lucky we are to have met him,' he growled in a cockney bass.

Having commandeered the bunks area, Kingsley slept soundly on a mattress stuffed with fragrant heather. Exhausted, Willum crashed out in the armchair. Sometime in the night, however, he woke. Moonlight pouring through the portholes showed that the sofa, on which Kansas and Mr McCool had fallen asleep, was empty. Voices were coming from up on deck. Pulling the duffel coat he had found in the hold closer, Willum crept to the hatch.

'Shoot, big fella,' Kansas was saying. 'What's it like?'

'Already told you,' Mr McCool growled.

'Tell me again.'

'Freedom is what it's like, Kansas. Freedom.'

'*Freedom.*' Kansas savoured the word. 'Kind of lonely, though, up there at the top of the world, Big Mac, in all that snow, with no birds, and no –'

'No birds? You ain't lived till you've seen the Arctic terns playing in the air.'

'Arctic terns?'

'We call them our *little wanderers.*'

'Nice name. *Little wanderers.* Say, what you call them that for?'

'Cos every year they fly from the bottom of the world to the top and back again.'

'Why do they do that?'

'Have to. Carry the sun in their beaks, don't they. If the *little wanderers* didn't fly to us in summer, then we'd never have any sun, and if they stayed wiv us *all* the time then them at the bottom would always be in the dark. That's why the tundra summer's so short, yeah? The journey from one end of the world to the other takes the *little wanderers* so long that they've hardly reached us up top before they have to be thinking about setting off for the bottom again. Always wandering. Me mum had a story about them –' Mr McCool broke off, turned to where Willum hid, and sniffed suspiciously. The boy held his breath. 'Who's there?' the bear rasped.

'Oh, tell me again about what it's like on top of the world, Big Mac,' Kansas begged in a dreamy voice, ignoring Mr McCool's question. 'Wasn't life a touch drab? I mean all that ice, ice, ice.'

Mr McCool's sudden deep, tender chuckle took Willum by surprise. He'd never heard the bear sound so gentle.

'Drab? That's *exactly* where you're wrong. Come summer there's flowers everywhere you look, dragonflies an' all, berries, herds of reindeer. Before . . .' The bear's voice cracked. 'Before I was snatched off of the ice, me and me mum used to lie in the cotton grass and watch the bees. Listened to the curlews singing an' all.' The bear grew as dreamy as Kansas. 'Most loveliest sound in naturedom. When you hear the curlew sing, you know everyfing's gonna be all right. One of me mum's sayings, that.' Mr McCool squelched a soft belch. 'All them apples is repeating.'

Kansas clapped his paws excitedly. 'The great white forever. I can't wait to see it.'

'But you ain't going up top. We're setting *you* free first, Kansas, remember? That's the plan. Drop you off before we head for the cold zone. Take it from me, you wouldn't like it there: your fur's too thin. Yeah, we'll be getting *you* home first.'

'*Home.*' Kansas laughed but Willum wondered if there was something hollow in the sound. 'Plenty of time before we come to that, big fella. Plenty of time. Now, tell me more about the great ice lands. Winter can't be much fun. A single night lasting for months, nothing to do but lie in the den.'

'Noffink to do?' Again that deep, tender laugh. Carefully lifting his head up through the hatch, Willum could see the black gem of the bear's nose in the moonlight. 'Icebergs is the best playgrounds in the world, little fella. And don't forget the dancing.'

'Dancing?'

'Wiv the *skittery-glittery.*'

'*Skittery-glittery*? Shoot, what's the *skittery-glittery*?'

'Ain't I never told you about the *skittery-glittery*?

Imagine the whole night sky flashing and roaring wiv colour. No words describe it. And when she dances, we dance wiv her, dance wiv the *skittery-glittery*.'

Willum's eyes narrowed. Did Mr McCool mean the northern lights, the aurora borealis? Silence fell, broken by an odd, whispering little sound, which drew Willum further out of the hatchway. The bear was humming a strange tune. Moonlight caught the tusk round his neck as he swayed from side to side. His great paws seemed to gently claw down the moon and stars. Wonderstruck, both Willum and Kansas stared at the sky-dancing bear.

'Well, it's somefing like that anyway,' Mr McCool faltered, falling back on all fours. Nose pointing to where Willum was listening, he scented deeply. 'That two-legs is on the move,' he rasped.

'Still won't trust him, huh?' Kansas asked. 'The grudge must run deep.'

'Deep as the eternal ice, little fella.'

'And here was me hoping you'd be friends. Can't you at least talk to him?'

'What you on about?' All the gentleness drained from Mr McCool's voice. Willum watched the bear shake his broad head. 'You've forgotten your own history, little fella, otherwise you wouldn't be talking about being friends wiv a human being.'

'But Willum's different. He's –'

'Answer me this: where was you born?' Mr McCool interrupted.

'In the zoo,' Kansas replied.

'And what was you doing there, you being otherwise perfectly adapted for a life on the great grasslands?'

The prairie dog hung his head. 'Great, great, great grandpappy Kansas got himself trapped.'

'And who laid the trap?'

'A human hand,' Kansas admitted.

'A human hand,' Mr McCool echoed. 'And don't you forget it.' He spread his talons. 'You can see my claws, yeah? You can't on a two-legs, but it don't mean that they're not there.'

'I know just as well as you the harm humans can do, Big Mac,' Kansas said. 'But I've learnt something new. They can do good too. Look at Willum, he's –'

Mr McCool cut in again. 'Oh, I've looked at him all right, and I've seen one thing: he walks on two legs.'

'Does two legs *always* have to mean bad, large lad?'

'You ask your greatest grandpappy. You ask . . .' Mr McCool sighed. 'You ask my mum.'

Pulse drumming in his temple, Willum listened to the bear padding away down the new deck.

'Hey,' Kansas called, scurrying after him. 'Large lad.' But Kansas didn't know what to say. Instead, he looked up at the glimmering night sky. 'Shoot, where did all those stars come from? There were never that many back in the zoo.'

To his surprise, Willum heard Mr McCool begin to chuckle. 'They were there all right, Kansas, we just couldn't see 'em.'

'Why you laughing, big fella?' Kansas asked.

'Don't you see what it means?'

'No.'

'They can't do everything. Can't have it *all* their own way. Humans can hide the stars, but even they can't steal them.' The bear's chuckle tailed off.

'What is it now, Big Mac?'

'All coming back to me, Kansas. What me mum taught. The polar bear way of looking at the world.'

'What do you mean, large lad?'

'Look up, little lad.' Mr McCool lifted his healing paw and picked out a constellation in the sky. 'That's the Whale. See her tail?'

'I see it,' whispered Kansas.

Willum looked up. He too could make out the shape of a whale in the ocean of the stars.

The paw picked out another constellation. 'That one there's the Arctic Fox, little fella.'

'Shoot, you can see her ears, big fella.'

Willum's eyes widened as he also found the fox.

'And there's the Raven and the Wolf, and over there you've got the Walrus; watch out for him.'

'You couldn't miss him.'

In the night sky high above his head, Willum saw a silvery walrus.

'When he shines clear, bad weather's coming,' Mr McCool said. '*Walrus ear, storm near.* Another one of me mum's sayings. Oh yeah, they're all up there somewhere. All the tundra animals. And, of course, there's *himself*, his nibs. See him, that single star, the brightest of all?'

'I see him,' whispered Kansas. Willum nodded to himself, gazing at the bright Pole star blazing in the sky. 'Say, who's he?' Kansas asked.

'Us,' Mr McCool replied. 'That's a polar bear – well, his nose. We call that star the *Bear's Nose*. You can always see a bear's nose, even in a blizzard. Black on white, innit? Yeah, all coming back to me.'

Willum was gazing at the stars when he became aware of a sound. Where was it coming from? It was so tender and pure that it seemed the stars themselves were singing. Then he realised, it was Mr McCool. Entranced, he listened as the bear sang about the sun in the *little wanderers'* beaks, the *skittery-glittery* and the sorrow of exile.

'For pity's sake, knock it off!' Kingsley shouted from below. 'I'm trying to get some sleep, not listen to some booze-cruise karaoke.'

CHAPTER 6
They Might be Giants

The next morning, leaving Kingsley to work on repairs, Mr McCool, Kansas and Willum set off further inland.

'And don't come back without substantial supplies,' Kingsley ordered. 'We'll need more than a few apples if we're going to reach your precious Arctic.'

Equipped with bracken antlers to keep the worst of the midges at bay, the foraging party soon reached the orchard and continued along the course of the burn. 'Have you noticed, we seem to be following some kind of path,' Willum told Kansas. At that moment, the prairie dog stopped dead. There was a boot print in the mud.

'Human,' Mr McCool snarled.

Kansas's little snout quivered. 'And one that's on

121

the big side. In fact, on the *very* big side.'

Mr McCool leant down and sniffed round the mud. 'Cold as ice,' he muttered. Lifting up on to his hind legs, he scented the air. 'Noffink on the radar neither.' He landed back on all four paws and turned to Willum. 'Hope no one round here is finking about doing a bunk and raising an alarm. Cos if anyone tries, I'll open them up like a chimp wiv a banana.'

'Hey, Big Mac, you're frightening me as well,' Kansas murmured. He narrowed his eyes at the huge boot print. 'A giant foot. As if we haven't got enough to be worrying about.'

Willum placed his own foot in the print. It was more than three times his size. He felt the hairs on the back of his neck lift.

'Let's turn back, large lad,' Kansas urged. 'Anyone wearing a boot that size isn't going to notice if he stands on a prairie dog.'

But Mr McCool was already walking on. 'Told you. No humans within a caribou's canter of here. Anyway, you heard the cat. We need supplies.'

The path grew wider. There were more of the gargantuan boot prints. Reaching a large stream,

Kansas, Mr McCool and Willum crossed a footbridge, hefty and wide enough for a lorry. The broad path led them to a fir wood where the air was sharp with resin. A wall as tall as a castle battlement showed itself beyond the trees.

'Ah well, too bad we can't go any further,' Kansas said, skittering back down the path. But Mr McCool had broken from the trees and was heading for a wooden door in the towering wall. 'What's the matter with him?' Kansas moaned.

'Isn't curiosity part of a bear's nature?' Willum asked, but even as he spoke, the height of the tall walls made his breath run ragged.

Kansas shook his head. 'Curiosity isn't the word for it. Oh no! Would you look at that!'

Mr McCool had shouldered the door down and was disappearing within.

Hurrying after him, Kansas and Willum found themselves inside a walled garden full of fruit bushes and well-tended vegetable plots. But this was no ordinary kitchen garden. All the fruit and vegetables were huge. *Everything* was huge. Willum had to jump up to touch the handle of a garden fork pronged in the soil.

'Still no scent of danger, Big Mac?' Kansas asked nervously.

Mr McCool sniffed deeply. 'Clear as ice.' Digging into a vegetable bed with a back paw, the bear unearthed potatoes the size of pumpkins. He took a suspicious bite, then wolfed down the lot. He lifted some carrots, the size of marrows, and ate every one, then he tore down a bean stalk, as tall as a tree, and swallowed the huge pods. He finished with a belch.

Willum felt a touch on his foot. Kansas ran up his body and on to his shoulder. 'What you thinking, Androcles?'

'I was thinking . . .' Willum lifted a hand to stroke the prairie dog. 'I'm just thinking that this isn't like a book.'

'Huh?'

'Real-life adventures, I mean. You can't just close the page and come back to them later.'

'Is that good or bad?'

But before Willum could answer, Kansas gave a joyful yip, scampered down to the ground and darted over to a patch of loose earth. 'Oh, this is good,' he cried as he began digging. 'This is perfect. This is real dirt!' And, forgetting that he'd ever been afraid, Kansas had soon gone from sight.

As Mr McCool filled the sacks with vegetables, Willum went over to the garden shed. It was the size of a house. Massive padlocks and chains webbed the door; a colossal bench stood under the window. Climbing up on to the bench, Willum peered inside the shed. Through the dusty panes thick with cobwebs, he could see wide shelves filled with nails the size of arrows. The hammers hanging from a wall would have needed someone from his *Treasury of Greek Heroes and Myths* just to lift them. A coil of twine was thick as a boa constrictor. Hooked on a rafter, the old tweed jacket would have fitted someone with shoulders even broader than Mr McCool. Willum was staring at these things in wonder when a face loomed up on the other side of the glass. He reeled back in shock.

It was only Kansas.

'Howdy, Willum,' the prairie dog called through the glass. 'I've tunnelled a way in.'

Hearing Kansas, Mr McCool came over to investigate. He lowered his head and barged the shed door down. Willum followed him inside. Mr McCool had reared up on his hind legs and was scenting the jacket with his glistening nose.

125

'Odd,' he said. 'Human, but *more*. Ain't fresh. No one's been here for a while.' He looked at Willum. 'What's going on?'

For a few seconds Willum couldn't reply, astonished that Mr McCool was speaking directly to him. 'They might be giants,' he managed to say.

Kansas blinked. 'Giants?'

'Big, *very* big people.' It was the only explanation that Willum could think of.

Shaking his head, Mr McCool turned to Kansas. 'What's the two-legs on about?'

'I don't know,' replied Kansas.

'But giants are only in stories,' Willum faltered.

'And just what are these *giants* like?' Kansas asked, little snout trembling.

Willum thought back to his old picture books. 'Cruel. They used to frighten me.'

'Surprise, surprise,' growled McCool. 'Cruel humans.'

'They're not human,' Willum said. 'Actually, they hate us. In fact, they eat people. They eat *anything*.'

'What a load of cobblers,' Mr McCool rasped. 'He's just trying to scare us. Only he ain't learnt that noffink scares *me*.'

'Well, it scares *me*,' said Kansas. 'Let's get out of here before any *giants* come along.'

But Mr McCool wasn't listening. His nose had caught something deep within the shed. Pushing past some hanging scythes, he disappeared into the shadows. There was a clatter and clash, a tangle of snarling, and then he reappeared triumphantly with a trumpet-sized object. It was a meerschaum pipe, the kind used for smoking strong tobacco.

'Bingo,' Mr McCool cried. 'Now all I need is the bark.' His nose greedily tested the air. 'Where is it?' he demanded of Willum. 'Where's the bark?'

'Bark?' Willum asked, taken aback by the bear's sudden mood swing. 'Do you mean tobacco?'

'I mean where's the stuff you burn to make smoke?' Mr McCool snapped. 'Ain't had a smoke since we broke out.'

'Hey,' said Kansas. 'I thought we'd left all that behind in the cage. Thought that was the old you. You know how it makes you cough. Come on, big fella, throw that away. Let's get the sacks and go.'

'Ain't going nowhere yet, little fella.' Mr McCool's nostrils flared. 'I spy wiv my little nose somefing beginning wiv tasty.'

The bear's nose led them to another door in the far wall. Still carrying the pipe, Mr McCool barged open the door on to a row of greenhouses, each as big as a barrack. Behind the glass grew hothouse fruit and vegetables, their colours blazing. Mr McCool slipped inside one of the greenhouses.

'Stone the Arctic skuas,' he complained, staggering back out a few moments later. 'Hot enough to melt an iceberg in there. Worth it though,' he added, licking the seeds from his snout. 'Perishable goods,' he explained. 'No good for storage, they'll go off. Here try one.'

He threw the others a strawberry each. Willum took a bite. A fountain of juice burst against the roof of his mouth. 'Like a peach,' he said to Kansas.

'Now that *is* tasty,' the prairie dog laughed, mouth full.

'Got this an' all,' Mr McCool declared, sniffing a long, thin red vegetable. It was a chilli pepper, and he devoured it all in one go. There was a moment's silence then he began to whimper. 'Hot,' he moaned. 'Flames. Burning. On fire!'

'Over here, Mr McCool,' Willum said, pointing to a huge watering can.

Mr McCool thrust his head inside the can and drank until he'd washed away the burning chilli.

'That's better,' he sighed. But when he lifted his head again the watering can came with it. He cuffed and snapped at it, shaking his head with all his might. 'Won't come off,' he yelled. Panicking, he rolled over and butted the can repeatedly against the ground, but nothing would shift it.

'Keep still, big fella,' Kansas urged. 'Let Willum help.'

As Willum reached out, Mr McCool's growl throbbed inside the can like a swarm of wasps. Hands brushing the beautifully soft pelt, Willum grasped the watering can. He twisted it gently, easing it off inch by inch.

Mr McCool gave a high-pitched whine as his head popped free like a cork from a bottle. Stunned, he gulped air. His eyes rested gratefully on Willum for a moment. 'Fanks,' he grunted. Then, shaking his pelt, he stalked off down a gravel path.

As Willum followed with Kansas, he could still feel the bear's fur in his fingers.

The path took them to an avenue of overarching yew trees. A very large sign was hammered to one of the trees. It said: KEEP OWT.

'What's that all about?' Mr McCool demanded suspiciously.

'It's a warning,' said Willum. 'At least, I think it is.'

'What's it say?' Kansas asked.

Willum read the sign out loud.

Mr McCool hmmphed and continued along the avenue.

'Shouldn't we do what it says, Big Mac?' Kansas called after him.

'Nah,' Mr McCool replied, lumbering on.

The others followed him.

A little further ahead there was an even larger sign: STRICTLEE NO ADMITANCE, ESPECIALLY NOT THEE.

'All right, all right,' said Kansas when Willum had read it out. 'We get the message.' He scampered back down the avenue. But still Mr McCool didn't follow. 'Big Mac,' Kansas urged. 'I've got a real bad feeling.'

'Can't stop now, little fella,' Mr McCool called. 'On the razzle, innit. A spot of mooching, yeah? Pilfering, ratching. *Got* to have a proper look around.' Mr McCool nodded his broad head at Willum. 'What does the two-legs think?'

Willum met Mr McCool's eyes. They held a

twinkle of excitement, and Willum felt it pass into his own. 'Let's have a shufty,' he said.

Willum regretted his words almost immediately. As they emerged from the avenue, a vast, ramshackle mansion rose from a moat ahead of them. Towers and chimneys fingered the sky like sea stacks; ivy clung to the crumbling stonework; battlements grimaced; tortured gargoyles screamed silently down at them. It was just like one of the giant's castles in Willum's old picture books.

'*Trespassers will be persecuted,*' he said, reading the words on a billboard standing in the moat. 'I think it should be "prosecuted".'

Kansas danced anxiously in a tight circle. 'Big Mac, please, time for –'

Mr McCool picked up his friend. 'Have I ever let you down, little fella?' Kansas shook his head. 'Exactly. Now, I'm telling you, the only fresh scent of two-legs is this one here.'

The drawbridge across the moat creaked under the polar bear's weight as he made his way over. Through the wooden slats, Willum could see, far below, carp lazing in the green water like a school of sharks. His stomach tightened like a fist.

'Here, you take the little fella,' said Mr McCool, handing Kansas over to Willum. Then, with a bellow, he hurled his weight against the castle door. A deadened clang echoed within. The bear tried again and again, until, finally, the door creaked open.

With Kansas on his shoulder, Willum followed Mr McCool into the mansion. Avoiding an array of mousetraps large enough to garrotte an unsuspecting prairie dog, the boy walked across a tiled hallway.

'Look,' whispered Kansas.

Willum looked up at the high ceiling to where the prairie dog was pointing. Cobwebs hung from the distant chandeliers like tattered shrouds. Dust coated the tapestries on the wall. Mr McCool scented the air for the bitter tang of tobacco, then bounded up a huge flight of stairs.

'Look out, Big Mac,' Kansas yipped.

Axe at the ready, a colossal, armoured figure guarded the first-floor landing. Mr McCool rose on hind legs, but his nose found only metal. A swipe sent the suit of armour tumbling, its clatter echoing through the seemingly deserted mansion.

'Wait for us, large lad,' Kansas called as Willum

hauled his way up the giant stairs after the bear.

They wandered through room after lavish room. Everywhere, huge, plush divans jostled with massive chaise longues and other titanically luxurious furniture. An immense golden harp stood in the corner of one room. Willum wandered over and was peering at the glittering strings when a cry of delight sounded out.

Mr McCool had jumped on to a four-poster bed and was wallowing in its sumptuousness. Giggling, Kansas leapt up after him. Laughing and shouting, they bounced as though on a trampoline.

'Come and have a go, Androcles,' Kansas cried.

Tentatively, Willum climbed up. The high spirits of the others were infectious, and he began to bounce too. Higher and higher they sprang, until the pillow and mattress split in a snowstorm of goose feathers. Mr McCool was in midair when his nose picked up the scent he'd been searching for: fresh tobacco.

Rolling off the bed, Mr McCool grabbed the pipe and followed the smell. He bounded up another flight of stairs and then another, until he was right at the top of the mansion. In the attics, he found piles of cheeses and hams swinging from the rafters.

Chomping his way through this storehouse, Mr McCool followed his nose to the bail of brown leaves standing in a corner.

'Sorted,' he cackled, clawing out a hunk of tobacco and stuffing the huge pipe full. A dense cloud of smoke was soon drifting through the attic. 'This is the life; *this* is freedom. Whatcha say, Kansas?'

There was no reply. Kansas wasn't there; neither was Willum.

At that moment, an angry shout boomed round the stately manor like a crack of thunder. 'FOUND YOU, YOU GRUBBY LITTLE TRESPASSERS!'

Shell-shocked, Willum stood on the first-floor landing with Kansas trembling in his arms. The shouting figure standing on the tiled hall below was big – very big. In fact, no two ways about it: he was a giant. Boots colossal as a pair of Rottweilers, legs like young tree trunks, he wore a battered tweed jacket and green corduroy trousers roped at the waist. Jellyfish eyes pulsed from underneath a cloth cap on a head high as a lamppost. As he held up a hand, his long, sharp fingernails glinted like daggers. 'TRESPASSERS WILL BE PERSECUTED,' the giant boomed.

Still holding Kansas, Willum sprinted down the landing, yanked open one of the many doors leading off it and plunged inside. The room was dark.

'Hole in the wall,' Kansas cried. He jumped to the ground and darted away. 'Over here, Androcles.'

Willum felt his way over. The hole was too small for him. Heavy footsteps shook the stairs as he feverishly searched for another hiding place. The landing trembled, the door was thrust open and a huge, ogre-shaped silhouette fell across the room. Willum threw himself under a bed.

'FEE-FI-FO-FUM, I SMELL THE PUKE OF TRESPASSING SCUM,' cracked the giant. 'DUG UP MAH TATTIES, SCRANNED MAH STRAWBS AND NOW THEY'VE BROKEN INTO BIG 'OUSE O' ME LORD'S. NEE RESPECT FOR PRIVATE PROPERTY.' Giving an ugly guffaw, the giant strode into the room. 'OH, I'M SORRY, MAH MISTAKE,' he said with mock politeness. 'THOU MUST BE NEW LORDS O' T'MANOR. WHY ELSE WOULD THOU JUST WALTZ INTO T'PLACE LIKE SHEEP INTO THEIR PEN? WHEN DIDST THEE BUY T'ISLAND OFF 'IS LORDSHIP, THEN?'

Peering through cobwebs thick as lace, Willum scanned the room for other exits. There weren't any. The vein on his temple throbbed like a snake.

The giant was chortling as though someone had just told him the funniest joke in the world. 'WHAT'S THAT? THOU *DIDN'T* BUY T'ISLAND? THEE *AREN'T* NEW LORDS OF T'MANOR? SO WHY 'AVE THEE BEEN ROAMING ALL OVER T'PLACE? BECAUSE YOU'RE TRESPASSERS – THAT'S WHY!' The ogre strangled the laughter in his throat. 'IF THERE'S ONE THING I CAN'T STAND, IT'S TRESPASSERS.'

This last word was a roar of rage. Feeling sick, Willum watched the boots crunch towards his hiding place.

'I GOES AWAY FOR A FORTNIGHT'S 'OLIDAY AND WHEN I COMES BACK FROM ME JOLLIES, PACK OF SQUATTERS 'AVE MOVED IN. DIDN'T THEE SEE T'SIGNS?'

The floorboards beneath Willum groaned as the giant dropped to his knees. All at once he was confronted by the jellyfish eyes.

'A JUICY BOY. OH, MAH LUCKY STARS. WHEN WAS T'LAST TIME I TASTED A PRIME CUT O'

BOY? ON'T SCRAWNY SIDE MEBEES BUT A BOY, A BOY, A BOY!'

The giant lunged. Willum lurched away just in time as a filth-encrusted fingernail burnt a scratch across the top of his head. The ogre's tongue bubbled in excitement. Nose hair twitching like spider legs, he thrust his face right against the side of the bed and reached in again.

The lethal fingernails were heading straight for Willum's throat when he felt something cold on the floor. It was a sewing needle the size of a stiletto blade. In a single movement, he scooped it up and stabbed the groping hand.

There was a deafening scream. 'I'LL FLAMIN' WELL FLAY THEE FOR THAT!'

In his rage, the giant shunted the bed aside, revealing Willum crouching there with the needle. A boot lifted to crush him. With a yipping bark, Kansas darted from his hole.

The giant's pained anger became raucous laughter. 'WHATEVER NEXT? FIRST A TASTY LAD AND NOW A BARKING MOUSE.'

Quaking but defiant, Kansas yikkered at the ogre until, like the jaws of a spring trap, a sudden darkness fell over him. The ogre had tossed his cloth cap over the prairie dog.

'I'LL 'AVE THEE AS A LICKLE SNACK,' the giant said, snatching up Kansas. 'ROASTED LIKE A CHESTNUT.'

At that moment, an even louder shriek bellowed out as Willum plunged the needle deep into the giant's thigh. Thrown free, Kansas shot under a table. Willum scuttled over beside him.

The giant hobbled across and kicked the table away. 'NOW IT'S PERSONAL. I'LL PARBOIL THE PAIR OF YOU FIRST, THEN, JUST TO GET JUICES TO BURST, I'LL ROAST YOU IN YOUR OWN OIL.'

The grotesque fingernails reached out, but before the ogre could grab Willum and Kansas, a meerschaum pipe the size of a trumpet flew through the air and struck him on the wrist.

'Quick,' Mr McCool cried from the doorway. 'Hop on.'

Willum and Kansas rode Mr McCool down the landing. He took the stairs five at a time, but the giant slid down the banister and landed on the hall tiles just behind him.

'*THREE* TRESPASSERS,' he sneered. 'WHAT'S

THIS ONE? SOME SORT OF TERRIER DOG?'

Mr McCool set the other two down. 'Go,' he said.

'We can't leave you, large lad,' said Kansas.

'Run for it,' Mr McCool roared.

Picking Kansas up, Willum sprinted across the tiles and out into the daylight.

Mr McCool sized up his opponent. Body weight equal or superior to his own, the ogre's main weapons were his fingernails, almost as lethal as walrus tusks. Shaking up his fur so as to appear even more solid, Mr McCool rose on his hind legs. A goose feather fell from his pelt.

'HAST THOU BEEN ROLLING ON 'IS LORDSHIP'S FEATHER BED?' the giant screamed.

Swaying his body and head threateningly, Mr McCool clawed the air – the deadly predator shimmer.

The giant spat. 'I WAS MISTOOK. YOU AN'T A DOG. YOU'RE A SHEEP, A RAM, A TUP.'

At the top of his lungs, Mr McCool bellowed the polar bear war cry.

'WOOF, WOOF! IS LICKLE DOGGY BEGGING FOR HIS SUPPER?' the giant mocked.

Mr McCool flopped back on to all fours. With a

touch of his tusk for luck, he tucked his body into a ball of pure muscle and hurled himself forward.

Crump! The giant toppled like a beanstalk.

Willum was running down the yew avenue with Kansas on his shoulder when Mr McCool caught up with them.

'Climb on,' the bear cried.

'You made it, Mr McCool!' Willum cried in joy.

Heart pounding like a prairie tornado, Willum held Kansas in one arm and clutched the scruff of Mr McCool's neck with the other. They thundered down the yew avenue, rumbled past the greenhouses and shot back through the walled garden. Despite the danger, Willum felt an odd elation growing inside him. The bear beneath him no longer felt like a captor.

But their peril wasn't over. Mr McCool lumbered out through the door in the wall only to find his way blocked by a group of huge shepherds and shepherdesses, each almost as big as the giant back in the mansion. With them was a herd of immense sheep, the size of the bear himself. The monstrous shepherds raised a howl as loud as a storm at sea. 'TRESPASSERS! TRESPASSERS! TRESPASSERS!

CHAPTER 7
The Great Escape

Kingsley cast a satisfied eye over the ship. Sometimes he even surprised *himself* with the sheer magic of his genius. The tide was out and he stood on the rocks, studying the strengthened keel. *Almost* perfect. He just needed a bit more wood. Where were the dunderheads? They'd been gone all morning. He worked on, but by afternoon the others still hadn't returned. 'Typical,' he said. 'One just can't get the staff.'

Much as he'd love to simply sail off by himself, the ship was too heavy to handle alone. He trudged up the rise of land to chivvy them on. No doubt they'd be lazing about somewhere. Following their tracks, he passed the orchard and continued along the burn. At the first boot imprint in the mud, he stopped. His tail wagged with displeasure. With humans about, one would have to be careful. Especially humans that size. Very few of them were like this Willum boy; Simple Simon he might be, but he was good-natured enough.

Cautiously, Kingsley crossed the bridge, pushed on through the woods and came to the towering wall. A flock of colossal sheep was penned against it.

'Hmm,' he reflected. 'Not the kind of scenario that invites closer inspection.'

Just then he spotted polar bear paw prints leaving the cover of the trees and heading for the wall. Behind the sheep, he could see a door. He sighed. Of all the foolish, fat-headed stunts to pull! Shaking his head, Kingsley dodged through the sheep to where a pear tree grew against the wall. Stealthily, he scaled it.

The first thing he saw on the other side was the huge vegetable garden; the second was a pair of even huger humans. Kingsley flattened himself.

'I'VE HOG-TIED T'TUP AND LOCKED HIM IN'T SHED,' the largest of the two giants said. 'T'OTHER TWO TRESPASSERS I FOUND ARE OVVER WEAK TO CAUSE BOTHER SO I'VE 'UNG 'EM LIKE

HAMS. I MENDED T'DOOR AN' ALL. GUARD 'EM WELL, NEICE BUMBA.'

The young ogress wore a bonnet and a long dress. She carried a floral crook. 'ARE WE 'AVIN' 'EM FOR DINNER, UNCLE GOLIGHTLY?'

'AYE, LASS. I'VE ASKED T'REST OF T'LADS TO STOP FOR SUPPER BEFORE GOIN' BACK TO THEIR OWN ISLANDS. FRESH MEAT *AND* WE'LL CRACK OPEN A HOGSHEAD O' ALE. GREAT WAY TO END OUR 'OLIDAY, EH? A REAL WELCOME 'OME PRESENT. OH, NEICE BUMBA?'

'YES, UNCLE GOLIGHTLY?'

'DON'T TOUCH THE BOY MEAT.'

'CAN I POKE 'IM?'

'NAY.'

'PROD?'

'NAY.'

'LICK?'

'NAY, NIECE.'

'WHAT ABOUT THE FUNNY MOUSE THING?'

'NAY.'

'TALKING TUP?'

'IF THOU SO MUCH AS SMELL THAT MEAT, I'LL 'AVE A SMELL O' *THY* LIVER. NOW, GUARD

'EM WELL. I'M OFF TO JOIN T'OTHERS AND LIGHT T'COOKING FIRE.'

Kingsley darted back down the wall and bolted through the woods to the ship. Well, if the zoo-two and their human companion insisted on putting their head into a lion's den, what could *he* do about it? The only thing for it was to get away as quickly as possible. Taking up his tools, he began to build a raft. It wouldn't take long to make, and once out at sea he'd soon find another ship. Any amount of rowing was better than facing what he'd just seen.

With a thick rope wound round his whole body like an anaconda, Willum dangled from a rafter in the shed. At first, the rope had burnt and bitten, but now he just felt numb. Kansas hung beside him, eyes closed. Only the occasional pained wrinkle of his nose showed that he was still conscious.

Drawing on all his reserves, Willum managed to say: 'Kansas, I've got a joke for you.' No reply. 'What did one rock pool say to another?'

Kansas opened an eye and tried to smile. 'Don't know,' he croaked. 'What did one rock pool say to another?'

'Show us your mussels. Get it? Mussels and muscles. Mussels are –' Willum faltered under a wave of pain. 'It wasn't as good as one of yours.'

'Shoot,' Kansas said in a small voice, 'I don't want to be eaten.'

Tied even more tightly than the others, Mr McCool lay on the shed floor below. He couldn't even move his head to chew at the thick rope binding him. This was all his fault; he'd been too busy searching for the tobacco to scent the giant humans. But, not only that, he should never have persuaded Kansas to escape with him in the first place – the prairie dog had been happy enough in the zoo. He had bullied his friend into coming because he hadn't wanted to go alone, and now the little fella would never see the prairies. If Mr McCool could have moved his head, he would have hung it low in shame. 'I'm sorry,' he groaned.

'What for, large lad?' Kansas whispered down.

Mr McCool's voice was a husked shred. 'If it wasn't for me you'd . . .'

'Hey, if it wasn't for you I'd still be in that zoo, staring at the bars,' Kansas interrupted, snout trembling. 'If it wasn't for you I would never have seen *the wild*. If it wasn't for you I wouldn't have the best friend in the world. And made a new one too.'

The bear choked. 'Don't say that.'

'It's true. Big body, big heart. That's you.'

Disguising his sudden sob as a roar, Mr McCool tried once again to break the rope holding him. But it was no use. With a bitter sigh, he lay back in defeat. Through the corner of his eye, he peered up at Willum hanging beside Kansas. What was it about this boy? Right from the start, he hadn't been able to hate him – not *properly*. And now, was he really beginning to actually *like* him? Perhaps he shouldn't have kidnapped him, perhaps he ought not to have taken him hostage.

Kansas's warning yip cut through his thoughts.

The giantess was pressing her face against the shed window. 'MEAT, MEAT MEAT!' she chanted discordantly, saliva running down the glass.

Peering at the grotesque face, made even more repulsive by the way it was squashed against the glass, Willum's mind reeled. Was there no way out? In his desperation, his thoughts turned to his *Treasury of Greek Heroes and Myths*. Hadn't one of the heroes also been captured by giants? Yes, Odysseus and his companions, on their way home from Troy.

Willum's aching, numbed body stirred with life as he recalled Odysseus's escape. 'Kansas, Mr McCool, don't worry,' he declared suddenly in a firm voice, surprising even himself. The eyes Mr McCool turned on him were dull with despair. Kansas had begun shaking in shock. 'I'm going to get us out of here,' Willum continued. 'I've got a plan.'

The raft was finished. A basic model, but sufficient. Pity about abandoning rat boy and his pals to such a sticky ending, but what could he do? Kingsley shrugged. That was the way with zoo animals; they just couldn't cut it in the wild. Humans as well. He'd almost begun to like them too. Those three oddball no-tails had treated him better than just about everyone else life had thrown him up against. Except, that is, for his first owner, his only owner, the kindest person he had ever known.

Kingsley wagged his tail; it was one of his rules never to remember his wonderful owner. There was no room for sentiment in a castaway's life.

Throwing his cushions, deckchair and a few supplies on to his hastily constructed raft, Kingsley dragged it into the water, climbed aboard and began to row. Soon the island lay on the horizon behind him, slender as a cat's tail.

Exhausted after his labours, Kingsley settled down for a well-deserved nap. A little sleep would build his strength up for all the rowing ahead. But his sleep was not restful. An old dream lay in wait, a bad one: a recurring nightmare in which a kitten is being drowned in a barrel of water. With a soft, choking yowl, Kingsley woke. For a while he struggled to get his breath back, as if water had been filling *his* lungs. This was not *just* a nightmare; it was a memory.

Motionless in the raft, fur flat and thin, Kingsley recalled how the cruel man, whom he thought was going to stroke him, had thrust him into a barrel of water. Kingsley heard again his own piteous mewls as the iron hands held him down, felt once more the water bubbling up his nose as his paws kicked weakly against the sides of the barrel. If it hadn't been for the little girl with hair as wonderfully ginger as his own, Kingsley Tail would have been dead as a stone.

Kingsley smiled at the thought of how the girl had braved the tattooed ruffian and whisked him to safety. Then his smile faded. In *his* hour of need, he'd been rescued, but now, when he'd had a chance to do the same for others, he'd thought only of saving his own skin. Was it too late?

Picking up his oars again, Kingsley rowed with all his might. His luck was in. A following wind sprang up; hidden currents ushered him. Then there it was, the grey island butting its rocky forehead against the sea. On Kingsley Tail went, into the teeth of danger.

Evening shadows were falling as Kingsley crept back on to the tall wall. Bumba, the young giant shepherdess, still had her face pressed against the shed window, tunelessly singing: 'MEAT, MEAT MEAT!' The ragged braying laughter of the other shepherds and shepherdesses rang out from somewhere further off. The cat peered across the walled garden to where he could see a huge stately home. On a lawn in front of the mansion, a circle of giants danced round a bonfire.

A moment later, Bumba heard a deep voice, which seemed to be that of her Uncle Golightly, say to her: 'Bring us a sack of spuds, will thee?'

'WHAT ABOUT GUARDING T'MEAT, UNCLE GOLIGHTLY?'

'Never mind that,' said the voice. 'Just bring us t'tatties.'

'WHERE ARE THEE?'

'Cooking fire; now hop to it.'

Bumba hurried over to the vegetable patch and began digging. Having filled a sack with potatoes, she headed for the cooking fire.

Seeing that his ventriloquism had worked perfectly, Kingsley shot down into the walled garden. In no time he'd found Kansas's tunnel and squeezed his way into the shed.

'Felicitations, hopeless oafs,' he greeted them.

'Kingsley!' Willum cried. Just when he thought he could bear it no longer, the cat had come to their rescue.

'Nice to see you too, dunderbread boy, but next time get Rentokil to make his tunnel a little wider. I thought my whiskers were going to be pulled off back there. Hear that, Cheeser?'

But Kansas was locked in shock; he couldn't reply.

'How did you get past the giant?' Mr McCool demanded.

'No time for chit-chat, hearthrug.' A quick glance showed Kingsley what he had to do. Leaping on to a shelf he nudged a pair of huge shears to the floor. He grabbed them and started sawing away at Mr McCool's bonds. He hadn't finished when they heard the giantess coming back.

'Bumba,' Kingsley roared, throwing his disguised voice once more.

'IS THAT THEE AGAIN, UNCLE GOLIGHTLY?'

'Aye, back at cooking fire, bring us some beans.'

'BUT I'VE JUST BROUGHT THEE TATTIES AND THOU SAID THOU DIDN'T WANT OWT. TOLD ME I 'AD TO GO BACK TO GUARD T'MEAT. TOLD ME YOU'D KICK ME UP T'BEHIND IF I LEFT T'MEAT ALONE AGAIN.'

'I'll kick you up t'behind good and proper if you don't get me mah beans.'

Jumping up on Mr McCool's head, Kingsley peered through the window to see Bumba picking a basket full of beans before hurrying off to the cooking fire. But Mr McCool still wasn't free when they heard Bumba coming back.

'Where's mah parsnips?' Kingsley demanded.

There was no reply.

'Bumba!' Kingsley cried. 'Fetch me some –'

'YOU'RE NOT MAH UNCLE GOLIGHTLY! AND

YOU'RE NOT AT COOKING FIRE.'

Kingsley sprang behind a cylinder of slug pellets as the huge, bonneted head burst into the shed. *If ever I get out of this alive*, he promised himself, *I will never, ever perform another unselfish act.*

'YOU MISERABLE TRICKSTER TRESPASSER,' Bumba hissed at Willum. 'I'M GOING TO ROAST YOU EXTRA SLOW FOR THAT.' With a gargle, she reached up for him.

'It wasn't him,' Mr McCool blurted.

The giantess swung round. 'WHO WAS IT THEN?'

'Me,' Kingsley said, unable to stop himself.

With a shriek, Bumba turned in Kingsley's direction. But she couldn't see the cat behind the canister. Thrusting aside tins of nails, she began to rifle through the shelves.

'You're looking in t'wrong place, lass,' Kingsley called, as though from the other side of the wall. 'I'm with t'sheep.'

'DAFT HAP'ORTH,' Bumba mocked, running from the shed over to the wall, 'FANCY GIVING THEESELF AWAY LIKE THAT.'

At last, Kingsley severed Mr McCool's rope.

'Ta,' the bear grunted, stretching his limbs.

'Comprehensive thanks and praise to follow, O monosyllabic one,' Kingsley grinned. With stunning grace, he sprang up the shelves to the rafters and, in a skilful flurry of sharp claws, unpicked the rope binding Kansas. 'Catch,' Kingsley called.

'Caught,' Mr McCool replied, Kansas safe in his hands.

'And another one,' Kingsley called, freeing Willum.

Mr McCool caught Willum and placed him gently on his feet, but the boy's legs buckled and he sprawled to the ground.

'I can't move,' Willum said, a wave of panic building inside him. 'I can't feel anything.'

'You just need to get your blood circulating again,' Kingsley said. He helped Willum up and walked him across the shed.

Kansas's chin and forepaws were shuddering uncontrollably.

'Don't worry,' Mr McCool soothed, rubbing the prairie dog's legs back into life. 'Used to happen a lot in the zoo, after a long day lying in the same position. Don't you remember? We called it the *invisible chain*.'

'*The invisible chain*,' Kansas stammered.

'Bumba's back,' whispered Willum.

'Situation remains perilous,' said Kingsley.

'Willum's got a plan,' Mr McCool blurted.

'The dunderbread boy with a plan?' Kingsley said. 'I knew he couldn't be as stupid as he looked. But do you trust him, hearthrug?'

Mr McCool nodded. 'And I don't fink he's so stupid,' he added. In the midst of his terror, Willum felt a flush of happiness.

'You get the plan rolling,' Kingsley said. 'And I'll buy us a few minutes.' And with that he squeezed himself back down the tunnel and out of the shed.

'Over here,' Kingsley summoned the giantess, who was just about to go back to the shed. Bumba hurtled over. 'Now I'm here,' the cat taunted, darting away before the ogress could reach him. 'Here. *Here*. Over here.' A game of deadly hide-and-seek ensued. Round and round the shed Kingsley trotted, evading Bumba's heavy tread. Dizzy, she staggered away. Kingsley backed slowly round to the door.

'GOT YOU,' Bumba cried, appearing behind him. A length of garden netting fell over the feline. 'CAUGHT MESEL' ANOTHER DIRTY LITTLE TRESPASSER.'

Like a fish in a net, Kingsley was scooped up.

Back in the shed, Willum and Kansas had recovered. 'What's the plan then, Androcles?' Kansas asked.

'Put the ropes back on so it looks as if you're still tied up,' Willum urged Mr McCool. 'Then wait for my signal. Kansas and I will look like we've fallen.'

'Giant coming back,' Kansas cried.

Bumba burst into the shed. 'THAT'S ALL OF YOU NOW.' She held up the net. Kingsley peered at them helplessly through the mesh. 'EH?' she demanded, seeing Willum standing there with Kansas in his arms. 'HOW DID THE PAIR O'THEE GET FREE? UNCLE GOLIGHTLY'S KNOTS ARE TIGHT AS NIGHT.'

Willum forced himself to look the young ogress in the eye. Would Odysseus's trick work for them too? He began shaking as though he were terrified, which wasn't so very far from the truth.

'Don't worry, we won't try and run away,' he began. 'We're too frightened.'

'YOU WANT TO BE.'

'Besides, you're too clever for us to outwit.'

Bumba chuckled. 'I AM, AREN'T I?'

'Anyway,' Willum continued, now making his

teeth chatter. 'The ropes were so tight they were marking my wrists – marking the meat. We wouldn't want Uncle Golightly to think you'd taken a bite, would we?'

The giantess peered at the weals on the boy's arms. 'NO, WE WOULDN'T,' she admitted suspiciously.

'So if you just let me and my friend stay here quietly without the rope, we promise not to try and get away.'

'ALL RIGHT. JUST SO LONG AS BIG WHITE TUP'S STILL TIED. BUT I'LL NOT LEAVE THEE AGAIN.'

Willum cleared his throat. Despite the danger, he felt a thrill of excitement. Was this how Odysseus felt?

'Are you really called Bumba?' he asked.

The giantess nodded. Willum forced a snigger.

'WHAT'S SO FUNNY?' Bumba demanded.

'Why not go the whole hog and just call yourself *idiot*?'

As she strode angrily towards him, Willum could feel Kansas's heart beating like a sparrow's wing.

'Mind you,' he added quickly, 'you're not the only one with a ludicrous name. You'll never believe what I'm called.'

'WHAT?'

'My name is *Nobody*.'

'*NOBODY?*'

Willum made himself smile. '*Nobody*.'

'HA-HA-HA!' Bumba's laughter shook the cobwebs and rattled the slug pellets in their container. 'THAT'S T'STUPIDEST NAME IN T'WORLD.'

'You haven't heard what the polar bear's called yet.'

'BEAR?'

'I mean the tup. He's called *It-doesn't-matter*.'

Now Bumba's laughter bounced the nails on the shelf.

'And the other one –'

'T'FUNNY-LOOKING MOUSE?'

Willum nodded and held up Kansas. 'This funny-looking mouse is called *Oh-just-forget-about-it*.'

Despite his quailing heart, Kansas pulled his funniest face.

'JUST-FORGET-ABOUT-IT!' The ogress laughed until tears rolled down her cheeks. She held up the net. 'WHAT ABOUT T'TINY TIGER?'

Willum peered at the imprisoned Kingsley. 'Tiny tiger's called *Get-lost-you-fool*.' Willum waited until Bumba had stopped shrieking with hilarity. 'Bet you can't wait to start,' he said.

'EH?'

'Tuck into the tup and tiny tiger, munch mouse, bite boy.'

Bumba's tongue flopped out and bubbled like a ready-meal in a microwave. 'OH STOP, YOU'RE MAKING ME HUNGRY. I AN'T 'AD A PROPER MEAT FEED FOR AGES.'

Drunken shouts drifted from the cooking fire.

'They sound hungry too,' Willum pointed out.

'THEY'RE GREEDY BEGGARS. IF I DON'T LOOK SHARP, THEY'LL WOLF THEE DOWN BEFORE I EVEN GET A BITE.'

'That doesn't seem fair.'

'IT'S ALWAYS T'SAME. I DO ALL T'WORK LOOKING AFTER 'IS LORDSHIP'S ISLAND, AND UNCLE AND T'OTHERS DO ALL THE SCOFFIN'. SPECIALLY IF THERE'S OWT IN THE LINE OF A DELICACY LIKE THEE. THEY WERE LIKE THAT ON 'OLIDAY AN' ALL.'

Willum steadied his voice. 'Why don't you get yourself a little taste while you can?'

Mr McCool stirred in alarm, Kingsley clawed at the net and Kansas's heart took flight, but Willum held firm.

'BEEN TOLD NOT TO.'

'Who's to know?'

'THEE, FOR A KICK-OFF.'

'But I'm *Nobody*.'

'THAT'S TRUE.' Bumba scratched her bonnet with a lethal fingernail.

'Why not just take a little bite?'

'AN ITSY-BITSY ONE?'

'You deserve it,' Willum coaxed.

'AYE, 'APPEN I DO.'

'How about this for a delicacy?'

For a moment Willum couldn't force himself to hold out his arm; how easily he might lose it if the timing wasn't perfect. But the feel of Kansas's beating heart gave him the courage. There was nothing else for it.

Bumba reached out, took Willum's arm between finger and thumb, and squeezed. 'FEELS SO FRESH,' she moaned.

Closing her eyes, the ogress prepared to bite. Willum left it for as long as he dared, then: 'Now!' he yelled.

With a growl that shook the shed, Mr McCool hurled himself at Bumba. Like a monster bowling pin she staggered back into the recesses of the shed. With a clatter of tools, Kingsley, released by Willum, sprang after the giantess and clawed her to the floor. Mr McCool threw himself in the air and landed belly to belly with the ogress, squashing the air from her like a whoopee cushion.

'Nice plan,' Kansas gasped as he ran with Willum through the door in the walled garden. The sheep were still penned there. 'What's next, Androcles?'

'Noffink complicated,' Mr McCool said. 'You lot get on me back, and we run for it.'

They followed Mr McCool's plan. Knocking his way through the sheep pen, they sprinted for the woods. A loud baa-ing broke out. The flock had taken fright and bolted. Mr McCool galloped over the footbridge.

They hadn't got much nearer their vessel when they heard Bumba's cries for help. 'UNCLE GOLIGHTLY, THEY'VE ESCAPED.'

'WHO'S ESCAPED?' Uncle Golightly boomed like a cannon from the cooking fire.

'NOBODY,' Bumba yelled.

'THEN WHAT ARE YOU BOTHERING US FOR?'

As the shipmates ran on, Bumba shouted: 'UNCLE GOLIGHTLY?'

'WHAT NOW, LASS?' her uncle grumbled.

'THEY'RE GETTING AWAY.'

'WHO'S GETTING AWAY?'

'IT-DOESN'T-MATTER.'

'GOOD, WE'RE BUSY.'

Golightly and the other ogres began cavorting drunkenly round the fire again. But once more they were interrupted.

'FOR T'LAST TIME, WHAT'S THEE WANT, BUMBA?'

'THEY'RE MAKING THEIR GETAWAY.'

'WHO IS?'

'OH-JUST-FORGET-ABOUT-IT.'

'EH?'

'AND GET-LOST-YOU-FOOL TOO.'

'WHAT DID YOU CALL ME?'

With shouts of rage Golightly could be heard tearing his way to the walled garden. Bumba shot away through the door leading to the greenhouses. Willum listened as Golightly and his cronies tore after her.

Mr McCool nodded. 'That'll hold them for a bit. Nice one.'

'Certainly not as stupid as he looks,' added Kingsley.

'He's the brains of this outfit,' Kansas laughed.

'I wouldn't go that far,' Kingsley said. 'But there were some nice touches. Good voice work. All in all, not bad for a novice. But let's not hang about here. Come on.'

Willum was laughing with Kansas as they ran away. But their relief was short-lived. They hadn't quite reached the orchard when a thunder of voices broke behind them like a storm. Willum looked over his shoulder to see the posse of giants brandishing their crooks. Golightly and his gang were on their trail.

'What now?' Kansas asked.

Willum felt the others waiting for his answer. What could he say? The giants hadn't given chase to Odysseus.

Mr McCool breasted the hill. The boat lay at anchor in the sea below, but the giants were closing in. Between the shipmates and their vessel stood the sheep, who had stampeded along the shore.

With a sudden laugh, Willum clapped his hands. He'd just remembered another one of Odysseus's tricks. 'Underneath,' he cried. 'Everybody underneath Mr McCool.'

'You're joking,' said Kingsley.

'It's the next bit of the plan,' Willum cried.

'Now what?' Mr McCool asked, when the others were clinging to his midriff.

'Mingle with the sheep, Mr McCool,' replied Willum.

The giants had arrived at the brow of the hill. 'WHERE ARE THEY?' one of them gasped.

'CLEAN DISAPPEARED,' another stammered.

'MUST BE SORCERERS,' a third cried.

'IDIOTS,' Golightly thundered. 'T'TUP'S JUST HIDIN' IN'T FLOCK. I'LL SOON CAP 'IM.' And with his crook he set to separating the flock, sheep by sheep. 'YAN, TAN, TETHERA, METHERA . . .' he counted.

Golightly was halfway through the flock when Mr McCool nipped a ewe lightly on her rump. With a braying baa, she sprinted off, followed by the rest of her sisters. The great woolly flock broke up, galloping in all directions.

'THE SHEEP, GATHER THE SHEEP!' the giant shepherds and shepherdesses cried, giving chase here, there and everywhere.

Hidden once more in the confusion, Mr McCool

was loping towards the shore when Kingsley sprang free. 'What are you doing, moggy?'

'You'll see,' Kingsley returned. He darted across the heather. 'Don't go without me,' he called.

'But the giants might come back at any moment,' Willum shouted.

'You go to the ship,' Kingsley commanded. 'I've one or two bits of last-minute shopping to do.'

Mr McCool swam to the ship with Willum and Kansas on his back. Anxiously, they waited for Kingsley to return.

'Where's he got to?' Mr McCool demanded. The tide was going out; soon they'd be beached. 'That flamin' moggy,' the bear growled. 'That big-headed tabby –'

'Tabby ahoy!' Kansas interrupted.

Kingsley stood on the beach, waving. Alongside him was a huge wheelbarrow attached to a sheep. The barrow held not only the sacks of vegetables they'd gathered but countless other odds and ends including a milk churn and a basket of eggs.

'Admit it, big fella – that's one talented tabby,' Kansas grinned.

Mr McCool laughed. 'Don't ever tell him, but I got

to agree wiv you. That moggy's a marvel.'

'And what about Willum,' Kansas asked. 'Isn't he a marvel too?'

'Behave yourself,' the bear said, but he winked at Willum. 'Now, what's that cat brought?' His nose probed Kingsley's haul from afar. 'Edible,' he pronounced, and leapt into the water.

Kansas turned to Willum. 'What did I tell you? The moment he first saw you I knew you'd be friends.'

'Yes, yes. On top of everything else I'm a bit of an entrepreneur,' Kingsley announced to Mr McCool as the bear reached the shore. 'Now, be a good tug boat and ferry this lot on-board. Hurry up, the tide's already turned.'

Loaded with sacks, Mr McCool headed back for the ship.

'Just wait until you've tasted my fresh cream cateaux,' Kingsley called after him.

The polar bear heaved all the goods on-board then came back for another load. On the third trip there was room for Kingsley too.

'And now let's skedaddle, before the super-sized buffoons cotton on,' the cat said.

'How do we skedaddle?' Kansas asked. 'The engine's gone.'

Kingsley smiled superiorly. He brought out the huge tweed jacket that had been in the shed and attached it to the mast with some giant braces. 'Voila! A sail.' He bowed with a flourish of his tail. 'Impressed? Of *course* you are. Up anchor.'

Just then, the sun came out to reveal the band of ogres streaming down the heather-clad hillside. 'TRESPASSERS *WILL* BE PERSECUTED,' roared Uncle Golightly. 'THAT'S WHAT T'SIGN SAYS. NOT TRESPASSERS WILL ESCAPE WILLY-NILLY, OR TRESPASSERS WILL SLIP THROUGH OUR FINGERS WHENEVER THEY WANT.' Reaching the sea, the giants waded out towards the ship.

'Who's got the next plan?' Kansas asked, eyes darting between his companions.

'Me,' said Mr McCool. Reaching into a sack, he scooped out a huge potato and hurled it with all his might. It struck Golightly on the head, and the giant stumbled and fell.

The shipmates cheered.

'Not bad for a bobtail,' Kingsley admitted.

But Golightly was already back on his feet. 'ME

OWN KING EDWARDS,' he seethed.

Mr McCool fired more spuds, and Kingsley, using the braces as a catapult, sent a hail of carrots. It slowed the giants' progress, but didn't stop them.

'MEAT, MEAT, MEAT!' they chanted.

'Cease fire,' commanded Kingsley. 'If we're serious about this voyage north, then we'll need those supplies.'

With the improvised sail bellying in the wind, the ship was moving out to sea, but not quickly enough. The ogres came nearer and nearer. Uncle Golightly was now wading up to his shoulders. 'Got you,' he shouted, grabbing the side of the boat.

There was a streak of ginger fur and a flash of claw. The giant howled with pain and sucked his scratched knuckle.

'Nifty work,' Mr McCool called over.

The rest of the giants arrived at the ship. With a roar, Mr McCool knocked one of them away whilst the cat clawed again. More howls thundered out. But on striking a third time Kingsley found his claws digging into leather: Golightly had put on a thick glove.

'HERE, KITTY, KITTY!' he mocked, lifting

Kingsley up by his lovely long tail.

Knocking a shepherdess away, Mr McCool sprang at Golightly. He was met by half a dozen huge crooks. They pinned him round the neck and paws. He rocked and shook, thrust himself back and forth, but couldn't wrestle free. Kingsley too was held fast. No matter how he kicked and spat and scratched, he was helpless against the gloved grip.

'SHOULD WE TAKE 'EM BACK T'SHED, UNCLE?' Bumba asked. ''ANG 'EM FOR T'FLAVOUR?'

'AND 'AVE 'EM ESCAPE AGAIN? NOT ON YOUR NELLY. LET'S SCRAN 'EM NOW, SUSHI STYLE. START WITH GINGER HERE. DROWN THE GRUBBY LITTLE TRESPASSER FIRST.'

'AND AH'LL 'AVE 'IS TAIL FOR A HAT,' Bumba laughed.

Golightly plunged Kingsley into the sea. The cat fell limp. He was facing death in water again. The first time he'd been saved by a miracle, but miracles don't happen twice.

'Big Mac, help Kingsley,' Kansas shouted. But Mr McCool was still pinned down. 'Willum?' Kansas begged.

Willum peered at the giant drowning the cat. What could *he* do?

At that moment a flash from one of the sacks caught his eye. It was a vanity mirror that Kingsley had purloined from the mansion; the glass was glinting in the sun. This time he didn't need any help from Odysseus. Snatching the mirror, Willum trained the sunbeam into Golightly's eyes.

'GERROFF!' the giant cried, trying to claw away the laser.

Willum ran to the bow, jumped on to the gunwale, and dazzled the ogre from close quarters. Blindly, the ogre swung out with his free hand. As Willum ducked, he lost his footing. His feet danced for balance, but he managed to keep the beam in Golightly's eyes and the ogre finally fell back, letting the cat go. Kingsley popped to the surface.

'Over here, Kingsley Tail,' Kansas barked frantically.

The giants turned on Willum. Dodging the grasping hands, he trained the beam in their eyes. They tottered back.

Mr McCool jumped free. 'Keep holding them back, Willum! I'll get Kingsley.'

But even as he spoke a cloud covered the sun. The laser died; the ogres closed back in.

'TRESPASSERS, TRESPASSERS, TRESPASSERS,' they chanted, trapping Mr McCool once more. 'TRESPASSERS WILL BE . . . CONSUMED!'

Golightly grabbed Kingsley again. 'BON APPETIT,' he cried as Willum looked on in despair.

'Now, think,' Kansas urged himself. 'What can *I* do? Too weak to fight, too puny to push anyone around, too small to . . . too small to be seen!' With a rallying cry, Kansas scampered up the mast. His head swirled at the height. 'Freedom vertigo,' he chuckled wanly as he pressed on. 'Shoot, if my cousins the flying squirrels can do it!' Reaching the top, he closed his eyes and leapt.

As Kansas fell, Willum ran at Golightly, heedless of his own danger. At the sight of him, the giant, who had just been about to take his first bite of Kingsley, burst into laughter.

Golightly was still laughing when he felt something land on his shoulder. The laughter became a shriek of agony. Whatever had landed on him had crawled up his jacket sleeve and taken a bite . . . and another, and another. The giant thumped where the pain was but only succeeded in winding himself.

Gnawing as he went, Kansas travelled across the giant's shoulders and down over his chest. Dancing in torment, Golightly thumped himself again and again.

'THEY'VE BEWITCHED 'IM,' an ogress cried, backing away.

'LOST 'IS WITS,' another shrieked.

'KNEW THEY WERE SORCERERS,' a third wailed.

Losing their nerve, the giant rabble broke for home. With a shriek, Golightly threw the cat free and followed.

'You saved me,' Mr McCool rasped at Willum.

'It was Kansas really,' Willum faltered.

Mr McCool's nose examined the boy. 'By the eternal snows, who *are* you?'

'Shoot, I guess he's your friend,' Kansas said, after leaping back on to the boat from the shoulder of the fleeing giant. 'And it's past time you realised it.'

Mr McCool shook his head in wonder. Willum reached out a hand. The bear stared at it, nose still working. 'What's that all about then?'

'It's what humans do,' Willum explained. 'Friends shake hands.'

171

'Bears don't,' Mr McCool returned. 'Truth be told, we're more likely to rip them off.'

'What do you do then?' Willum asked.

Mr McCool shrugged. 'Dunno.'

'Do what the rest of us do,' suggested Kansas.

A deep growl sounded out. Surprised by the sudden ferocity, Willum staggered back. All at once his fear of Mr McCool returned double fold, as though he were back in the zoo den. In a blur he saw the great head lumbering at him, teeth glinting. But instead of attacking, the gem of the black nose came to rest against his.

'Friends!' Kansas cried. Barking joyfully, he cartwheeled over the deck. 'I knew it, knew you could be friends. Friends, friends, friends!'

Mr McCool nodded. 'Friends.'

'Friends,' laughed Willum.

'Kingsley?' Kansas called in delight. 'Kingsley, come and see who've just made friends.'

But Kingsley was lying lifeless and limp in the water.

CHAPTER 8
Storm

Safe from the giants, the ship pulled out to deep water, but the crew was no longer celebrating. Heads bowed in silence, they were on deck, gathered round the body of Kingsley Tail. Willum stared numbly at the whiskers, marmalade fur and wonderful tail; how still they were now. He tried to blink away his tears.

'May he find his place to shine in the long winter sky,' Mr McCool intoned.

'May he blow free as the prairie wind,' Kansas murmured, eyes glistening with sorrow.

'May he dance wiv the *skittery-glittery*.'

'And fly with the geese beyond the Black Hills.'

Willum looked up to see the others peering expectantly at him. What could *he* say to mark the tragedy of Kingsley's passing? A picture from the beginning of the journey came into his mind. It felt right. 'May he flow with the river into the one, wide sea.'

Mr McCool nodded solemnly. 'And walk on the eternal ice and –'

'I'd rather not if it's all the same,' a feline voice declared. 'Bit cold on the old paws.' Coughing and spluttering, Kingsley sat up.

'*You're alive!*' Kansas cried.

'Ten out of ten for observation,' Kinglsey said, cleaning himself nonchalantly.

Willum gazed in amazement.

'Alive, alive, alive-o!' Kansas cried, sprinting round the deck.

'We thought you were . . . gone,' Willum whispered.

'Strictly speaking, the old chestnut of us cats having nine lives may be a myth,' Kingsley said loftily, 'but there's more than a grain of truth in it as a testimony to the feline resourcefulness.' Kingsley broke off. It was only now that it was sinking in. One minute he'd been underwater, saying goodbye to life, and now here he was. Miracles *did* happen twice.

He looked in wonder at the others. *Joy* lit their

faces. 'Thank you,' Kingsley said, unable to hide the crack of emotion in his voice.

'Shoot, you're one of us,' Kansas said. 'Part of the team.'

Kingsley felt a lump in his throat. How could he express his gratitude? How could he show them how he felt? 'Well, what are you waiting for, dunderheads?' he snapped. 'We've got a ship to run. This is no longer some land-lubbing canal barge. We're bound for the Arctic Circle.

There was a loud belly rumble. *'Hun-gery,'* Mr McCool said.

'Breakfast will be served in the morning,' Kingsley answered.

Mr McCool winked at Kansas and Willum. 'Nah. Can't wait till morning.'

'Listen, greedy guts,' Kingsley bridled, 'if you think I'm going to start cooking after all I've been through.'

'Want food, tabby.'

'I want never gets, shagpile.'

Mr McCool smiled. 'Welcome back, pussy cat.'

Kingsley bowed. 'Touché, hearthrug. Now, who's at the helm?'

'The helm?' Kansas asked. 'What's the helm?'

'The wheel, the ship's wheel? You know, the mode of steering a sailing boat?' Kingsley sighed in operatic despair. 'You don't have a clue, do you? I'll have to explain it *all* . . .'

By the time Kingsley had explained the rudiments of sailing, night had fallen. The cat yawned. 'Now we're on-board a proper sailing barque you can no longer be a mere rabble,' he announced. 'We'll have to take it in turns to keep night watch. Naturally I'll be excused tonight.' His tail lifted as though to test the breeze. 'The sail should be all right as it is. But if the wind changes you'd better let me know. By the way, I've curtained off the bunk area. The shagpile's snoring really is too much.'

'I'll take the first watch, then,' Willum offered.

Mr McCool shook his head. 'I'll do it. You deserve a rest.'

'It's all right,' said Willum. 'I want to. You see, now I'm part of the crew, I want to do my fair share.'

'You've already done that,' the bear said, 'but if you're sure. As it happens, I could do wiv a kip.' He winked at Kingsley. 'And a good old snore.'

*

Willum had never known a night so dark. The lantern hanging on the mast was a single eye of light in the vast black of sea and sky. The night was chilly too. The breeze pushed its sharp fingers through his duffel coat, but Willum felt warm inside. He was no longer a hostage. Smiling, he gazed up. The wind had blown away the clouds; the sky was full of stars. They were just as Mr McCool had described. The Whale with its tail, the Arctic Fox, and over there the Bear's Nose, the Pole Star, towards which they were sailing. What was that other constellation shining so brightly? Oh yes, Mr McCool had called it the Walrus.

Sensing someone else up on deck, Willum turned. Kingsley stood in the pale light of the lamp.

'These are for you, Willum.' He handed over a bundle: thick trousers, socks and a jacket. 'Actually, it's a rather good tweed,' Kingsley explained, pointing at the sail quietly whispering in the gloom. 'I had some left over. Put them on, then. Can't have you cold.'

'They fit perfectly,' Willum said, fastening the trousers.

'What did you expect? I'm a master tailor on top of everything else. I couldn't bear looking at you shivering. Fur-less as well as no-tailed. Not your fault, of course. Just a double disability. Now, don't mind my little joke. Warmer?'

'Thank you,' Willum said. Before he realised what he was doing he'd reached out and stroked Kingsley's head.

For an instant the cat's eyes closed happily. Then: 'It's time for straight talking, boy. Just exactly what are you doing on this boat?'

'What are *you* doing?' Willum replied.

Kingsley smiled. 'Let me put it another way then. You're far from home, Willum. Do you even know where you're going?'

The boy shook his head.

'I thought as much. A fellow traveller. You and I are not like Rodent Robert and Arctic Adam. They've got a destination. *We're* castaways. Explorers adrift on life's ocean.'

'Have you always been a drifter, Kingsley?'

'You mean have I always been a stray?' The cat smiled sadly. 'You may find this hard to believe, dunders, but like you I too once lived under a roof with central heating, ample food and a kind hand to stroke me.'

'You had an owner?' Willum asked in surprise.

'She was the kindest, loveliest, bravest . . .' Kingsley went on to tell of his rescue from the tattooed arms and barrel of water. 'I left six sisters and two brothers in that barrel, and only just managed to escape with my own life. She wasn't even half the brute's size, but she took him on. Punched and kicked and bit. Just like a cat.'

'So why didn't you stay with her?'

Kingsley's brow furrowed. 'The weeks after she saved me were the best of my life. I was her pet. She fed and cared for me. Provided limitless milk. But it couldn't last. You see, she was taken away from me. They moved house. I tried to get into the car with her as they drove away, but a boot kicked me out. It belonged to Mr Tattoos. I never saw her again.'

Kingsley told Willum how, forced to fend for himself, he'd taken to the streets. He recounted his early years as an alley cat, the fighting, the scavenging, the time spent at the stray pound, until finally he'd run away to sea.

Silence followed Kingsley's tale. The night wind was still freshening and the tweed sail filled restlessly. Above them the Walrus shone ever more

179

clearly. 'Well, that's *my* story. What about you? How did you set off on the wanderer's life?'

'It just sort of happened,' Willum replied.

Kingsley nodded. 'Chance, fate, destiny – that's what's brought you here. Brought us all. For some reason we were chosen.'

'I went to the zoo and fell into the polar bear enclosure.'

'And here was me beginning to think you weren't so stupid.'

'I don't know how it happened, really. I think it was his eyes. They seemed to draw me.'

'Ah, that old trick: the predator pull.'

Willum paused. 'He took me hostage.'

'*Hostage?* That doesn't sound good.'

'To help him escape. The strange thing is I'd just been thinking about helping him anyway. I'd wished that I could. And now, well, I'm glad it happened.'

'A strange destiny.' Kingsley studied Willum. 'But what about your family? Your mother and father, brothers and sisters?'

'I . . .' Willum faltered.

Kingsley's green eyes shone kindly. 'You don't

need to say. I can see it. *You're* an orphan too. Well, we two lost ones are comrades now.'

The pair were smiling at each other when a sudden gust tore at the sail. Willum looked up. In the sky, all but the Walrus constellation had been extinguished by cloud. *Walrus ear, storm near.* The old polar bear saying! Willum ran to the prow and peered into the night. He could hear a dull roar in the distance.

'Quick, we're in danger,' Kingsley cried. His caterwaul brought the others up on deck. 'Haul in the sail,' he commanded. 'Hurry up, there isn't a moment to spare.'

The storm broke. Hurling rain and malice, a gale wailed over them. A savage squall lifted Kansas clear off the ground. Willum leapt up and grasped hold of him.

'Batten down the hatches and go below. There's nothing we can do now,' Kingsley cried.

Down in the hold they watched jagged forks of lightning flash at the portholes. Timbers shrieking, the ship lifted and fell like a deadly fairground ride, sending the crew slamming against the sides. As though boiling under the heat of some unseen flame, the sea bubbled and spat and frothed. Cliffs of fizzing water crashed over the deck. It was only a matter of time before they would sink.

For a whole day and night the tempest raged. Then, at dawn, as suddenly as the storm had come, it left, like a wild stallion galloping away.

'We've been lucky,' Kansas declared as they re-emerged back on deck. 'Nothing's broken.'

'*Lucky*,' scoffed Kingsley. 'Yes, due to my ship-wrighting skills, I've saved your lives yet again.'

'Is it just me,' Mr McCool interrupted, 'or has it gone all . . . warm?'

Kingsley glanced knowledgeably at the sky, and nodded. 'We've been blown off course.'

''Ot,' the bear whimpered. 'Gone all 'ot.'

'I'm afraid the storm has swept us into tropical climes,' said Kingsley.

Not a breath of wind fanned the sail. From the bows, Willum stared out over a flagstone-flat sea. The air shimmered.

'Out of the frying pan into the fire,' Kingsley remarked.

'Dropped by the eagle, caught by a rattlesnake,' said Kansas.

'Too 'ot,' Mr McCool moaned. 'Too bloomin' 'ot.'

Mr McCool was paralysed by the heat. Willum tied a rope to the watering can, which Kingsley had grabbed from the walled garden, and threw it overboard. They hauled it back up and hoisted it on to the mast above where Mr McCool lay.

'That's better,' Mr McCool moaned as a yank of the rope created a shower. But the can was soon emptied. 'Again,' he panted. 'Again.'

'The novelty of this is going to wear off very quickly,' remarked Kingsley as they threw the watering can back into the sea. 'Why can't you just jump in yourself?'

'Can't move,' the bear moaned.

The long, hot hours passed in a torment worse even than any of those Mr McCool had known at the zoo. Night came, but the air remained thickly humid. He lay on the deck moaning, tongue lolling.

'For pity's sake shut up,' Kingsley cried. 'You're not the only fur-bearing mammal on-board. I'm hot too, but am *I* whinging?'

*

Next morning, it was just as sultry. Willum and Kansas heaved the sail down and made it into a gazebo to shelter Mr McCool from the sun. They took it in turns to fan him with a sack and pull the rope to give him a watering-can shower.

'So we're off course,' Kansas said nervously to Kingsley. 'How do we get back *on* course?'

The cat shook his head. 'We can't do anything without wind.'

Tempers simmered. It was so hot that no one could stand being in the hold. Kingsley cooked and then served lunch up on deck. Knowing how it annoyed Kingsley, Mr McCool ate straight from the pot.

'How dare you?' Kingsley exploded. 'You ignorant, lout-haired –'

'Shut your snout, you bossy, ring-tailed alley cat!' roared Mr McCool.

'*You* shut *your* snout, you great overgrown excuse for a West Highland terrier!'

'You orange, talentless tabby!'

'You bob-tailed, Old English sheepdog gone wrong.'

'You tiny tiger!'

'You stinking, belching husky!'

The cat and the bear squared up to each other.

'Wind!' Willum suddenly shouted. 'I felt a puff of wind.'

Everybody stopped and looked up in hope.

'Must have made a mistake,' Willum admitted after a while. At least his lie had stopped a fight. 'Kansas, have you got a joke?'

Kansas giggled. 'Been saving one up. Why do whales make the best teachers? Because they're always . . . because they're always . . .' Despite the heat, he hooted with laughter. 'Because they're always hanging about in schools.'

'Actually, it's a pod,' Kingsley corrected. 'If you're going to tell lame jokes, at least make them accurate.'

''Ot,' whimpered Mr McCool.

'I've had enough of this,' Kingsley said. Gathering his tools and some spare lumber, he climbed the mast and set to building a platform. When it was finished, he took up his cushions and other soft furnishings and scattered them around. With a sigh of relief he sank back into them. 'At last, breathing space from the riff-raff.'

The second day in the doldrums wore on with Kansas fanning Mr McCool, whilst Willum, barefoot, took the wheel. Every movement sent a drop of sweat pattering on to the deck. As Willum stood at the helm, he could hear Kingsley muttering.

'What did I do to deserve being stuck here with a stinking polar bear?' the cat grumbled. 'Things can't go on like this. To think that I, Kingsley Tail, famed throughout the seven seas . . . and yet here I am, a prince cast away amongst savages . . . I need an assistant . . . a buffer between me and that bear . . .'

Fresh hammering burst out from the top of the mast.

'He's putting up a sign,' Willum told Kansas.

'What's it say, Androcles?'

'*Situation Vacant*,' Willum read. '*A once-in-a-lifetime opportunity to work under the finest chef on the seven seas.*' He screwed up his eyes for the small print. '*You must be exceptional to work for the best.*'

'He wants someone to wash his pots and pans,' Mr McCool growled.

The tip of a long, ginger tail curved down from the daybed in the shape of a smile. But Kingsley's tail-smile disappeared as a shower of water broke over him. Having finally managed to crawl over to the bow, Mr McCool had rolled into the sea. 'That's better,' he groaned. 'Bit cooler.' He stayed in the water all afternoon.

'Got to think of a way out of this,' Kansas murmured to himself, standing at the wheel. Willum was down below, sheltering from the sun. 'The big fella can't stand much more. None of us can.'

He was wondering just exactly what could be done when he heard a sharp knocking on the deck. A large bird – something like a crow – was perched untidily on the gunwale. Head cocked, it was staring right at him, huge beak pointing like the barrel of a gun. With a great caw the crow flapped a pair of tattered wings and flew raggedly at Kansas. The prairie dog closed his eyes in horror.

But the bird wasn't attacking. She was just trying to perch nearer to him. She missed her footing and fell in a heap. Fluttering weakly, the bird tried to get up from the deck. She was clearly exhausted.

Kansas skittered over and helped her up. 'There you go, friend,' he said uncertainly.

With a deafening caw, the crow secured her perch on the gunwale. 'Friend?' she mused. 'I like that. It's not often that we members of the corvine community get such a warm greeting. If you don't mind me asking, ducks,' she asked, 'What *are* you?'

'I'm a prairie dog,' Kansas explained, returning the bird's smile.

'You're a long way from home, little bright eyes. Did you get caught in the storm too?' The bird shuddered. 'There I was flying with me flock one moment, and the next, *whoosh*, I'm blown here. Such heat. You haven't seen anyone else like me, have you? A whole load of us? I lost them in the storm. No? Thought not.' She sighed heavily. 'So, when do I start?'

'I'm sorry?'

'Why, what you done?' The great beak opened wide to expell a deafening, grating rasp of laughter. 'Nothing to be sorry about, little bright eyes. I've come about the job.'

Hearing the laughter, Willum looked up through the hatchway to see the large bird talking to Kansas. To his ear, her voice had the ring of a Brummie accent. And to think that when he'd first seen Kingsley he'd thought nothing could surprise him again.

The crow spotted Willum and began flapping and screeching in terror.

'Don't worry, friend,' Kansas said. 'Willum won't hurt you.'

'Where's its gun?' the alarmed bird cried.

'He doesn't have one. Willum don't kill.'

The bird's beak scanned Willum.

'A *nice* wild bird,' Kansas whispered to Willum. 'A new friend.'

'*Friend.* I really do like that word,' croaked the bird. She hopped hesitantly towards Willum, still keeping a safe distance. 'Are you his nibs then, the finest chef of the seven seas?'

Willum smiled. 'I think it's Kingsley you want.'

Kansas called up to the daybed. 'There's someone enquiring about the job.'

'Send them up,' Kingsley commanded.

The crow fluttered scrappily up to the daybed.

'What on earth do *you* want?' Kingsley demanded.

'The job, duckie.'

'There's obviously been some kind of mistake.'

'*Situation Vacant,*' the bird quoted. '*A once-in-a-lifetime opportunity to work under the finest chef on the seven seas*?'

'Oh, dandy,' said Kingsley. 'An agricultural pest that can read.'

'*You must be exceptional to work for the best,*' the bird finished.

'Well, that's me,' Kingsley conceded haughtily. 'But I very much doubt whether it's you.'

'Why not, flower?'

Kingsley scrutinized the raggedy, blue-black bird. 'Somehow the words *crow* and *cuisine* don't exactly trip off the tongue.'

A gust of raucous laughter caused Kingsley to flatten his ears. 'You are funny. But fish is just food, isn't it? If there's a piece of carrion within ten miles, this beak'll scavenge it for you.' The beak opened so wide that the cat could see the bird's tongue wagging.

Kingsley blenched. 'Please, don't do that. Look, I'm the world's premier piscatorial culinary genius, amongst other notable achievements, and you're . . . well, you're a crow.'

'That's where you're wrong, smarty tail. I'm a rook.'

'You might be a raven for all I care, but my personal assistants were most remiss allowing you on-board. This isn't the job for you.'

'*Who* is it for then, flower?' the rook asked.

'Frankly, someone with a little more style. I had in mind a frigate bird perhaps, or an albatross . . .'

'Oh, I can fly as prettily as any of them la-di-das. Just watch me.' With a flop of her frayed wings and a tearing screech to match, the rook careened up from the daybed, nearly knocking Kingsley down. But her attempts to glide gracefully went awry and she plummeted into the sea.

'Thank you so much for your interest,' Kingsley called down. 'Clearly rubbish dumps and sewer overflows are more in your line.'

The rook struggled out of the water and flapped away so heavily that her wings tickled Mr McCool's belly as he lay dozing on the sea.

'Say, Kingsley,' Kansas said. 'Couldn't we at least have invited her to supper?'

The cat shook his head. 'Encourage that kind of riff-raff and you'll never be rid of them.'

Another night passed. Still no wind, and still the heat lay over the sea as though an oven door had just been opened. The crew's store of spring water was running low.

'Can't go on,' panted Mr McCool.

Fanning his friend, the prairie dog tried to hide the worry in his voice. 'Say, Big Mac, got a new joke.'

Mr McCool shook his head.

'But it's a really funny one.'

'Nah.' The bear shook his head feebly.

Just then, in a great screeching whir, the rook crash-landed on the deck.

'Not her again,' Kingsley groaned. 'All the finesse of a toilet mop.'

'Hello, duckie,' the bird called up weakly. 'Job still vacant?'

'Look,' burst Kingsley, 'I may be forced to cater for a clientele with all the panache of a dustbin, but Kingsley Tail will never, I repeat, *never*, have a carrion bird for an assistant.'

As though she no longer had the strength to lift her head, the rook's beak tapped the deck weakly. 'Thing is, flower, I'm lost and I've been flying for ever so long looking for me flock.'

Kingsley was adamant: 'We already have enough gregarious vermin of our own on-board this ship. Go!'

Willum picked up the bird. 'Would you like something to eat, or to rest for a while?'

'That's very kind, but I know where I'm not wanted, ducks. Give us a boost.'

'Are you sure?' Willum asked.

'Don't worry about me. I expect I'll find me flock soon.'

Reluctantly, Willum threw her into the air. With a ringing caw, she clattered away, leaving a blue-black feather spiralling to the ground.

'I sure hope you're proud of yourself,' Kansas shouted up at Kingsley. The prairie dog danced furiously on the spot. Willum had never seen him angry before. 'Look at what you've done.' He pointed accusingly at where the rook was a failing black dot over the sea. 'The meanest, selfishest, stupidest . . .'

'For the sake of argument, I'll allow your first two epithets to pass, but your third! I, Kingsley Tail, who has achieved . . .'

'Seems what you've achieved is not caring a cuss for anyone except yourself. Shoot, no wonder you're cast adrift all alone in this world.'

Drowsy applause came from under the makeshift gazebo where Mr McCool lay.

'I thought taking in castaways was the first rule of the sea,' Willum added.

'Winged creatures don't count, dunderbread boy,' Kingsley said.

'Winged or not, that bird was in trouble and you sent her away,' snapped Kansas.

The rest of the day passed with the ship locked in the doldrums. Hearing the growing rumbles of Mr McCool's stomach, Kingsley stirred himself reluctantly. First he'd have to catch the fish, then he'd have to prepare them, all in the sapping heat. Not only that but he felt guilty about the rook. Maybe there *was* enough room on the ship for one more of life's drifters. He snatched up the vanity mirror. He may not *look* any different, but since falling in with Willum and his preposterous gang of no-tails he had begun to *feel* different.

'All right,' he cried to the ship in general. 'I was wrong. Happy now? I should have welcomed that bird, inelegant and inappropriate as she was.' Wearily, he descended into the hold.

'Hello, duckie,' a grating voice greeted him.

'I don't believe it!' Kingsley cried. 'Of all the audacity! Of all the sheer trailer-trash tenacity!'

'Freshly caught,' winked the rook. 'Smell the aroma.'

The cat inhaled and smelt the catch, piled high on

the kitchen surface. Despite himself, he began to purr.

'I've whisked some eggs as well,' the bird grinned. 'And used the apples to make a strudel.'

Kingsley had to admit it: the rook was as fine a pastry chef as he had ever known – except for himself, obviously. He peered at the bird. She'd lost so many feathers she barely looked capable of flight.

'The job's yours,' he said.

The rook gave a resounding cry. 'You won't be disappointed, ducks.'

'On one condition,' Kingsley went on. 'You refrain from the use of such ludicrous nicknames as *ducks* or *flower*. For your information, I am a highly evolved land mammal of superior sophistication, not some foolish aquatic fowl or weed of the wayside.

'Get away with you!' Opening her beak as wide as it would go, the rook laughed so loudly that the noise knocked Kingsley off his feet. 'What jollies we're going to have, ringo-tail. What high jinks and larks!'

Kingsley struggled out of the feathery embrace. Kansas and Willum cheered from the hatch. Even Mr McCool had dragged himself over.

'That's better, moggy,' Mr McCool said, sniffing the apple strudel.

'Knew you had a heart,' Kansas chipped in.

'Kindly refrain from drooling in my kitchen,' Kingsley returned, shivering at the sight of the bear's long, panting tongue.

'Say, what's your name, friend?' Kansas asked. The bird cawed loudly. 'Didn't quite catch that,' the prairie dog said. Again the rook opened her beak and cawed long and loud: a wild, swooping dance of noise.

'It sounds like a rookery,' Willum said.

The rook continued calling.

'No,' said Kingsley. 'Still not making any sense.'

The rook laughed. 'Well, why don't you just call me *Friend*?'

'Welcome aboard, Friend,' Kansas grinned. 'Our team's just got another player.'

CHAPTER 9
Voices from the Deep

Friend settled in quickly. Not only was she an expert fisherwoman and pastry cook, but she was a storyteller too. To distract the crew from the heat and their irritability, she told tale after tale of her rook family flock. But nothing could hide the seriousness of their situation. Only two barrels of water remained, and there was still no wind to blow them out of the doldrums. Rationing began. No sooner had Mr McCool received his daily ration than he gulped it down, immediately to be ravaged by thirst again.

Only Friend seemed to have any energy, and she continued with her tales.

'For the love of milk, shut up,' Kingsley roared. 'Who cares about the time Great-Auntie Blue Black flew higher than an eagle, or Cousin Croak followed the swallows as far as the pyramids? Who cares *anything* about the antics of a rookery?' He found some parsley to block his ears and fell sound asleep.

Next morning Willum was sitting listlessly at the prow of the ship when he felt something caress his face. He closed his eyes to make sure he wasn't imagining it. No, he really could feel a delicious breeze blowing. 'Ahoy, wind!' he called out.

With a yap of joy, Kansas lifted his snout. He too felt the air combing his whiskers. 'It's blowing,' he barked.

'A real flying wind!' Friend croaked, jumping into the flowing air.

'Praise the eternal ice,' Mr McCool rasped. 'We can get out of here.'

The breeze picked up. Leaping to his feet, Willum looked up at the tweed sail. It hung lifelessly as ever. Puzzled, he gazed out to sea. The water was calm: no wavelets, no little flecks of foam, no sign of the blow. Yet as well as *feeling* the wind, he could *hear* it through the rigging. Not only that: he could hear voices. The wind was carrying voices.

Their boat must have drifted near land, or was another ship hailing them? Willum ran to one side and then the other to investigate. He hurried to the stern. There was no sign of island or vessel, just the empty sea. Yet the voices were growing distinct, more insistent. Where could they be coming from? Willum felt the hair on the back of his neck shimmer like seaweed in a rising tide. Were they calling *his* name? He listened over the sudden bumping of his heart. Yes, there could be no doubt; someone was calling him.

All at once the sea began to bubble and fizz. A wave lifted from the foam and rolled slowly towards the ship. The voices were coming from the water.

'*Willum.*'

The boy was filled with joy. 'Yes?' he heard himself call back.

'*Willum.*'

Then he saw them – just shapes to begin with, like the white horses people glimpse in the surf, but as the wave came closer he could make out arms, legs, heads.

Delight fluttered inside him like a bird in a cage. 'What are you?' he shouted in astonishment.

'*Willum, where have you been?*'

Nearly at the boat now, the figures were clearly no mere foam shapes, but two distinct people. A man and a woman, they were walking on the water, their arms outstretched.

'What do you want?' he asked breathlessly.

'*You.*'

'Who are you?'

'*Don't you know?*'

Willum's hands started to shake. Although he had never heard them before, the voices felt familiar. Wasn't this how he had always imagined his mother and father sounding? The blood rushed at his ears. A gasp tore from him. Now that they were closer, he realised that their faces were familiar too. He'd often looked at them in the framed picture he kept beside the computer on his bedroom desk, taken only months before the fatal crash.

'*We've been looking for you for a long, long time, Willum.*'

'But you're dead,' he faltered.

'*Willum,*' they called again, reaching out. '*Our little boy.*'

Wild hopes raged through Willum like a fire.

Hadn't Kingsley spoken about being *chosen* to go on this journey, about destiny? Was *this* his destiny? Was this the reason for all these strange happenings? Was this *his* odyssey?

Almost choking with excitement Willum stepped on to the gunwale.

'*Willum, come,*' the kind-sounding voices coaxed.

'Mum, Dad!' With a ragged shout of joy, the boy jumped.

As though weightless, Willum seemed to hang in the air. He had time to see that his friends had jumped too. Beak wide open as a nestling, Friend spiralled dizzily upwards before plunging into the sea like a sooty gannet. Arms whirring drunkenly, the widest grin on his face, Kansas was also falling. Mr McCool teetered on the side of the ship, then he was dropping as well. But Willum was too euphoric to give much thought to the others. His parents were waiting for him.

After the peculiar slowness of his fall, the almighty splash on hitting the water was like an electric shock. He had been expecting his mum and dad to catch him. Looking about for them, he saw only a swarm of bubbles. Then he heard them again, some way below, calling his name. With a wild kick, he dived down.

When at last Willum reached the voices, the joy burning his heart turned to ashes. The well-loved faces of his parents dissolved in bubbles until all that was left of them was the lethal silence of deep water. Willum looked up in horror. The surface was a distant rumour of sunlight; he had very little air left in his lungs.

Kingsley, his ears blocked with parsley, woke later than the rest of the crew. Time to prepare another meal: where was he going to get the energy? Then he remembered the new staff. 'Friend,' he called, 'this is your big chance. I'm putting you in charge, temporarily. *I* need to concentrate. I've got very important work to plan, new menus to create.' And with that he fell back asleep.

When he woke again, he pulled the parsley from his ears. 'Progress report,' he called. No reply. Kingsley peered down from his daybed. The deck was empty.

Descending the mast, he darted into the hold. That was deserted too. The ship had been abandoned.

Back on deck, he stared over the placid sea. The ocean glinted like a mirror showing no reflection. Kingsley's tail drooped. Just when he thought he was beginning to belong somewhere, his so-called friends had ditched him. They must have hailed a passing ship. A wailing miaow ripped from his throat. Oh, it was his own fault. He'd broken the rules. Why had he let himself start to care about others? A fat tear plopped on the deck. He swatted it away angrily. Never again would he allow himself to be conned into friendship. Tortured by betrayal, Kingsley scanned the sea. What was that speck in the distance? No doubt the steamship for which they had deserted him.

Mr McCool grasped Willum by the scruff of the neck and hauled him up to the surface. Boy and bear plundered great tearing breaths of air.

'Got to get the others,' Mr McCool grunted.

Still fighting for breath as he treaded water, Willum watched Mr McCool dive. Despite the heat, a deathly chill made him shiver. How could he have been deceived so easily? It wasn't that long ago he'd read about sirens in the pages of his *Treasury of Greek*

Heroes and Myths. Evil spirits of the ocean, they lured sailors to their death. Now he knew how they did it. They enticed the sailors with words that they could not resist.

With a gasp, Mr McCool broke the surface once more. He was holding Friend. 'Here,' he said, placing the rook on Willum's head. Taking a deep breath, the bear dived again, his colossal body leaving behind a frail chain of bubbles.

'Where are they?' Friend croaked, clearly still bewitched by the sirens. 'Me flock, they're calling.'

'They aren't,' Willum said gently, still treading water.

'But there's a rookery,' the bird insisted. 'I heard it, high up in the lime trees.'

'It isn't real. There are no trees here.'

Friend croaked desolately as she too realised the siren's emptiness. 'Not real,' she whispered.

Willum looked around for Kansas and Mr McCool. Where the phantoms had walked, now rolled an empty sea. There was no sign of the ship.

Mr McCool creamed through the water: a living submarine. No longer an unhealthy zoo exhibit, his body was beginning to take the form and strength of a wild animal. The sea-ghouls had lured him by pretending to be his mother, but the bear had nurtured her voice so long in his heart that not even a siren could deceive him for long. Even before he hit the water, he had understood the trickery, and then his first thought had been for his friends. Now here he was nosing through shoals of bright-coloured fish, peering under waving sea plants. Where was the little fella? *Let me find him*, Mr McCool begged. *Let me drown but not him*. He was just about to return to the surface to get his breath for a third dive when he glimpsed the missing one in a shallow coral meadow, floating like a frond of kelp.

'Kansas!' he cried in a rush of air bubbles.

Sprawled in his daybed, sleep was proving elusive for Kingsley. Once again he scanned the sea. The speck had grown bigger. It wasn't a steamship at all. Was it . . . could it be . . .

'It's the hearthrug!' he cried. And weren't those smaller specks the others, perched on the floating bear's belly? Kingsley's thoughts span in confusion. Could he really accept that they'd discarded him like a fish bone? No! His friends wouldn't desert him.

Something must have happened whilst he lay sleeping with the parsley in his ears. And now they were in dire straits.

Hurriedly, Kingsley lowered his raft on to the sea. He filled an empty barrel with supplies and placed it on the raft. After just a moment's pause, he jumped overboard. With a wretched miaow he hit the water and, paws flailing, hauled himself on to the raft. 'Oh, for a pea-green prow,' he sang as he rowed with a wooden spoon filched from the ogres. The song soon died on his lips. His friends were a long, long way away. He needed all his energy to reach them.

Floating on his back, tortured by the heat, Mr McCool was approaching exhaustion. He'd managed to save Kansas, but he hadn't been able to find Kingsley. Shipmates perched on him as though in a battered lifeboat, the bear had been searching for hours. Even now he refused to believe that they'd lost the feline chef.

Punching himself in the nose to keep awake, he continued the search. He sniffed the air continually, but his nostrils only ever found salt. At last, like the others, he fell into an exhausted asleep.

As the crew slept under the stars of the tropical sky, Kingsley continued to row. His paws were cut to ribbons. His emerald eyes swept the darkness like a pair of searchlights, but they found nothing until dawn broke and they glimpsed a whitish mound glimmering on the deep. 'I'd know that great, greedy belly anywhere!' Kingsley cried.

Willum was the first to wake. 'Kingsley!' he gasped when he saw the cat nearing them in his raft.

The look on Willum's face told Kingsley all he needed to know. They hadn't abandoned him.

'Hurray for Kingsley, the king of cats!' Kansas shouted as he stirred, and leapt into the cat's arms.

'You marvellous tabby,' Mr McCool stammered.

'No slobbering, please,' Kingsley said, but his haughty tone quickly made way for a grin.

'The maestro moggy,' Friend laughed.

Dipping into the supply barrel, Kingsley distributed emergency water rations and some seafood delight baked the day before. The crew drank and chewed slowly, mouths and beaks blistered by salt and sun. 'What happened back there?' Kansas asked when they had eaten. 'I felt a prairie wind blowing, but when I went to it I found –' With a shudder, he broke off.

'Sirens,' Willum said. 'I think they must have been sirens.'

Kansas's little nose quivered. 'What are sirens?'

Willum's voice dropped. 'I suppose you might call them ghouls. They drown sailors by enticing them into the sea. No one can resist. Even Odysseus only survived because he had himself tied to a mast.'

'Who's Odysseus?' Kansas asked.

'A Greek hero,' Willum answered.

Kansas chuckled. 'Friend of Androcles, huh?'

Mr McCool's voice was small. 'Thought they were my mum.'

'Me too,' said Willum.

'Hey?' Mr McCool lifted his weary head.

'My mum and dad. I thought they were calling me. But it was only a memory of them. I haven't seen them since . . .'

Willum felt a tickle of fur. Kansas was running up on to his shoulder. They rubbed noses.

'Just a memory,' Mr McCool murmured gently,

peering at Willum. 'Seems me and you have got fings in common.' To cover his sudden emotion, the bear winked at the others and said: 'But what I want to know is, how come *you* didn't hear noffink, tabby?'

'Oh, a superior capacity to withstand mental manipulation,' the cat replied airily, removing a stray sprig of parsley from his ear.

Laughter burst from the others like a flock taking flight.

'How did you find us?' Friend asked.

'Night vision is another surprise in my bag of tricks. As well as oodles of gumption.'

Although Kingsley's arrival revived their spirits, it didn't change their circumstances. They were adrift on a vast ocean under an implacable sun. With no room for Mr McCool on the raft, he floated alongside. How they endured that day they would never know, but when the cat issued the last of the rations and night fell again, their ship remained lost. If they didn't find it soon, it would be too late.

'We can't have this,' Kingsley said to himself as the others slept heavily. 'We can't just give up.'

The moon laid its crystal pavement on the sea.

Kingsley rowed, his purr soothing the darkness. He might be castaway once more, but he was no longer alone. He looked at his companions. Asleep, Willum seemed even younger; a few freckles dappled his face like spots on a young animal's pelt. Friend perched beside the boy, head hidden in her breast, weary wings held out gingerly like a tattered cormorant. Kansas was curled right into Mr McCool's throat fur. Let them sleep. Who knew what tomorrow would bring?

Kingsley was still pondering their fate when he felt his wooden spoon hit something. He reached down and pulled up a branch. The sea around him was bobbing with greenery. 'Where there's a branch,' he whispered, tail fluttering, 'there's a tree, and where there's a tree . . .' Stifling his excitement, Kingsley waited for first light to confirm his hopes. The sun rose. There indeed was a distant coastline. With a shout of joy, he woke Kansas. 'Make the announcement, Roberto Rodent! I know how much you like such menial tasks.'

'Announcement?' Kansas yawned.

Kingsley pointed at the coastline and nodded.

'Land ahoy!' shouted Kansas. He jumped into

Kingsley's paws but, mistiming his leap, almost fell into the sea. 'Diggable, scoopable, more ahoyable than it's ever been before. We're saved! Land in view!'

CHAPTER 10
Lost . . .

'Looks steamy,' Kingsley pronounced as he gazed at the coast. 'Some kind of jungle.'

Mr McCool moaned. 'That's all we need.'

'Yes, well, you'll have to get used to it,' Kingsley said. 'It'll take me more than an afternoon to build a whole new ship. Look on the bright side, bulk boy, there'll be plenty of water and other supplies to fill that fat stomach of yours. Now, I can't see any natural harbours. Aha, there's a river. We'll row upstream until we find a mooring place.'

Kingsley rowed with renewed gusto. Soon the forest could be seen distinctly, and the steam rising from it. In no time at all they had reached the river mouth.

Tall trees festooned with creepers jostled right

down to the waterside on both banks. Brightly plumaged birds filled the air with song. With a screech, a parrot bulleted over them. Friend called out, but the other bird showed no sign of hearing her.

As the raft rounded a bend, a monkey troupe chattered and called to them from high in a mahogany tree.

'What they saying?' Kansas asked Willum.

'I don't know,' he replied.

'Not on talking terms with your kin, huh?'

Willum looked up at the monkeys, who stared back. He hadn't thought about it like that before.

Some boulders stood in midstream. Carefully, Kingsley slalomed between them. They were nearly through when the last rock lifted its head. The boulders were hippos! With a desperate flurry of his oar, Kingsley just managed to thrust them free of the huge animal.

The raft was now moving so quickly that it sent up sprays of water.

'Observation to make, ducks,' Friend said. 'We seem to be going *against* the flow.'

Willum looked at the river. The current appeared to be running in the normal way, to the sea, but when Kingsley stopped plying his oar, the raft continued to move upstream.

'Wild rivers are full of currents,' Kingsley told them.

'Some current,' Friend murmured.

'Hadn't we better be mooring?' Kansas asked.

'And just where would Vernon Vermin suggest we moor?' Kingsley gestured at the dense jungle. 'This place isn't exactly brimming with harbours and marinas.'

They reached a fork in the river. As Kingsley beached his oar and pondered the different ways, the raft edged up the narrower course. When he tried to row it back, the raft kept going upstream.

Kingsley shrugged. 'Seems our choice has been made for us.'

Another bend took them into a lagoon fringed by dense reed beds. The lagoon was carpeted with bright white lily-like flowers that gave off a strong scent. Leaning over, Kingsley picked one. Purring, he buried his nose in it. 'Now *that* makes a welcome change from odour-of-wet-polar-bear.'

'Bit cloying, if you ask me,' Friend cawed.

'Who cares about a smell,' said Mr McCool.

'It's so flamin' 'ot, and I'm flamin' thirsty and flamin' hungry.'

Spying a freshwater spring and a gap in the reeds, Kingsley rowed over to the shore and sprang on to land.

'Hope there are no crocodiles,' Kansas said anxiously, glancing about as Willum picked him up. 'Or any other inhabitant of the reptile house.'

'Have you noticed?' Willum asked. 'There are no birds singing here.'

'Just as well,' said Mr McCool, clambering on to dry land. 'They was getting on me wick.'

'And no monkeys,' Kansas added.

The crew drank deeply from the spring. Thirst quenched, Willum peered at the tall wall of reeds hemming in the lagoon. 'It's funny,' he remarked. 'But I feel as though we're being watched.' He moved closer to the reeds. '*Anything* might be hiding in there.' He was still staring suspiciously into the vegetation when a sudden scrunch and a slurp rang out, followed by a belch. Mr McCool was eating.

'What you got there, ducks?' Friend asked.

'This,' Mr McCool replied. He was standing in the shallows, holding up a large purple fruit, which promptly disappeared in two rapid bites.

'That looks nice,' Friend said, and with a flurry of her wings she hopped across the lily pads to where Mr McCool stood in the midst of a floating patch of purple fruit.

Despite his hatred of water, Kingsley too waded over and bit into a fruit. 'Cat's aren't normally frugivores but . . .' His words were lost in a deep purring.

'Tasty?' Kansas yikkered. 'Shoot, I'd like a bite.'

Willum carried Kansas to the lily pads, then he leant down and picked a fruit. It was lovely and cold to the touch. His mouth watered. The urge to bite into the soft purple pulp was so powerful that he staggered. The soft skin seemed to soothe away the hunger and thirst of the past days.

Kansas was already eating. 'Come on, Willum, eat up,' he cried, snout covered in juice and seeds. It's past de-lic-ious.'

Willum was just about to take a bite when an almighty splash made him drop the fruit. Mr McCool had fallen backwards into the water. Even as Willum looked, Kingsley too collapsed. Then Friend. Willum plucked her out of the water, but when he turned back to Kansas, the prairie dog was laid across a lily pad.

Willum rushed to each of his comrades in turn. Their eyes were wide open, but no matter what he said or did, Willum couldn't wake them. They seemed to have fallen into a strange sleep. Only their breath against his cheek showed that they were still living.

As he tried to rouse his friends, Willum felt his own eyes being drawn back to the fruit. Never had he wanted to bite into anything so badly. He lifted a fruit to his lips, opened his mouth and . . .

At that moment there was an explosion of screeching and chittering. Something sprang on to his back. He felt a lancing pain between his shoulder blades as though from the bite of sharp teeth. He yelled in agony. A small monkey leapt off him.

'Quick,' she shrieked. 'Quick.' Round her neck was a metal collar, from which dangled the broken length of a chain. The chain clinked as she hopped from foot to foot.

'What's happened to my friends?' Willum asked.

The monkey let out a howl. 'Too late to save *them*.'

'Why are they sleeping?'

'Sleeping? Sleeping? To sleep, you must wake.' She hung her head. 'This is a sleep from which no one wakes.' Her eyes peered at Willum. 'Get on your raft and leave while you still can.'

'I'm not leaving my friends.'

'You have to!' Chain rattling, the monkey danced frenziedly on Mr McCool's stomach. 'You don't know what happens. I do. Seen it before. Too many times. You will eat and then be lost too. Those who eat are always lost. And then, and then; oh, it's too terrible to say.' The little monkey, face full of sorrow, buried her head in her hands.

'Lost?' wondered Willum. 'What do you mean?'

'Look for yourself and you'll see.'

The monkey gestured at Kingsley. Willum leant down and gazed into the cat's eyes. As though looking through a green window, he saw the ginger tabby sitting on a red-headed girl's knee. The cat purred as the girl stroked him. A bowl of milk stood close at hand.

'Lost,' the monkey whined. 'Your friends are all lost. Look at the others.'

Willum picked up Kansas and stared into his large, wide-open eyes. In them he could see the rodent digging happily into a limitless grassland surrounded by other prairie dogs.

'And the bird,' the monkey murmured.

Through Friend's eyes, Willum saw a swirl of dots – her lost flock. There in the middle flew Friend herself, tumbling and playing with her clan through a windy sky above lime trees.

'Now, the large one.'

In Mr McCool's eyes the boy glimpsed an endless range of Arctic, and Mr McCool roaming free.

The monkey was weeping softly. 'Dreams of home. Wanderers always dream of home.'

'I don't understand,' Willum said.

'The only thing to understand is that you must go. The longer you stay, the more cruel will be the temptation.'

To his bewilderment, Willum found that he had picked a fruit. His knees buckled under a savage surge of craving. Despite the warnings, he *had* to eat; he couldn't resist. For a third time, he was just about to bite into the fatal fruit when, for a third time, something stopped him. From deep within the reed bed, a melody had begun to play, sweet but mournful, like the last hymn at a funeral. The monkey threw her head back in horror and, with a scream so piercing that Willum dropped the fruit, she fled. For a time Willum could hear her chain clinking until only the music remained. It reached him in pulses, now stronger, now weaker, like someone sighing. With a cry, Willum remembered the sirens, covered his ears and bent over double.

Quickly, Willum noticed two things. Firstly, he could still hear the music perfectly; secondly, it didn't *feel* like the sirens' song. Nothing was pulling or *bewitching* him. The music – a flute perhaps, or an organ? – was desolate rather than alluring. He wanted to get away from it, not closer.

Heart pounding, he pulled his fingers from his ears and waited. Nothing happened. No spell was being cast. He darted over to his friends, but they remained deep in their trances. The music continued. Perhaps this musician could help. Who else could Willum turn to for help? The monkey had gone. Taking a deep breath, he slipped into the reeds and headed for the melancholy melody.

The vegetation closed behind like a slammed door. Rushes lashed his hands and face as he toiled his way towards the music. Soon he felt as disorientated as if he were in a maze, or a labyrinth. *Labyrinth?* Didn't they often harbour unpleasant inhabitants, such as bull-like minotaurs? Swatting aside the unsavoury thought, Willum pressed on, the air growing ever thicker and more humid.

Perhaps he'd been in the reed maze for five minutes, perhaps an hour, when he realised that the music had stopped. Instead, he could hear a squeaking: a dry, repetitive cheep, as though from some large, flightless bird.

Willum halted. 'Hello?' he called. 'Hello?' Was there someone ahead? He peered hard at the sedge before him. Yes, movement. Something heavy and low-slung, something like a bull. And it was coming towards him.

As Willum watched the thing slowly approach, the squeaking grew louder. All at once he saw it. What he had taken to be a bull was – strange to say – some sort of trolley. The squeaking was coming from the wheels rolling through the dense vegetation. Pushing the trolley was a man.

'Please,' Willum called. 'You must help me. My friends won't wake up.'

Despite the heat, Willum shivered. Faint as a pencil

drawing worn away by time, the man passed through the reeds towards him like a shadow. He had no substance save for his eyes, which were a shining vortex of purple – the colour of the fruit. Eyes whorling, he seemed to be searching for something.

'I'm over here,' Willum said.

The shadowy musician stopped just in front of Willum, but stared beyond him as though at some reality only he could see. Taking hold of a handle on the trolley, he began to turn it with his ghostly hand. The sombre melody mourned through the reeds again.

It's a barrel organ, Willum realised. Attached to the organ was a broken chain. The monkey's collar! 'Whoever you are, please help,' Willum pleaded. 'My friends are asleep. They've eaten the fruit.'

Still grinding the music, the shadow set off with his barrel again, passing straight through Willum like a cold draught.

The hair on his head tingling, Willum followed. 'Please, my comrades are in danger.'

Suddenly, the ghostly organ grinder grew enraged. He grabbed the chain and whirred it above his head. Round and round the chain whirled then, suddenly, it lunged at Willum, only to pass harmlessly through him like a gust of foul air from a grave. Willum gave a loud cry. Countless shadowy figures were swarming around him: men and women, wearing all styles of clothes, from every country, age and epoch. Children too, and babies. Only their eyes held colour, and they blazed with the psychedelic purple of the fruit. Insubstantial bodies writhing, the shadows broke over Willum like cobwebs.

In blind terror, he ran. Faster and faster he fled, heedless of where he was going, not noticing that the ground was getting softer beneath his feet. Suddenly he found himself sinking to his knees. Before he had time to free himself, the mud sucked him deeper, up to his waist. With a desperate corkscrewing of his body he managed to pull himself on to firmer ground. Chest heaving, he stared at the quicksand which lay all around him. The barrel organ music was fading in the distance and the ghostly shadows were gone, but he felt no relief. He had run right into the heart of a swamp.

'Is he gone?' the little monkey whispered to Willum, her face appearing in the reeds.

Willum felt the blood rush to his ears in relief. He nodded.

'Follow me closely,' the monkey said. 'Tread only where I tread; stand only where I stand.'

A hundred questions flew through Willum's head. Yet there was no time to ask: his friends were in danger. With skilful steps, the monkey picked her way through the swamp. She moved quickly, often slipping from view so that if it hadn't been for the clinking of her chain, Willum might have lost her. Gradually the ground firmed until at last Willum found himself stumbling out of the reeds.

They had emerged on to one of the lagoon's hidden bays. Willum had to look twice to understand what his eyes could see. The bay was full of boats. Vessels of every description were moored tightly together: ancient ships with rows of oars, modern pleasure craft, galleons, brigs, prison hulks, trading clippers, yachts, even a ferry. Yet more craft were concealed in the reeds.

'They all come here,' the monkey explained. 'Sucked in from the sea, pulled up the river. Yes, they all come.'

Stunned, Willum was gazing at the secret harbour

when a wild hope flared in him. He ran along the line of lost ships.

'What are you doing?' the monkey called.

'Looking for something,' he shot back.

The monkey found him climbing up on to a ship. 'That one has just arrived,' she explained.

'It's ours,' Willum cried. '*Our* boat.' Everything he saw held a happy memory: the mast Mr McCool had raised; Kingsley's daybed; Friend's perch on the bow; the little platform placed at the ship's wheel so Kansas could steer. But his elation was already draining away. What use was the boat when those who had sailed it with him were lost? Willum was searching the hold when he felt movement. Coming back on deck he saw that the ship was drifting slowly out of the bay on to the lagoon itself.

'I have unmoored her,' the monkey said, holding up the vine which had held the ship at harbour. 'The current has found her – the *real* current – and soon the river will take you back to the sea. At last, one of the lost can return. One of the forsaken fleet can return home.'

'But I can't go without my friends.'

'Your friends are gone.'

'Where?' Willum's voice broke.

'Better not to know.'

'I *have* to. Look, there they are!'

Willum pointed to where his shipmates could still be seen lying where they had fallen.

The monkey shook her head. 'They have made their choice.'

Willum's face creased with bewilderment. 'Choice?'

'The fruit takes them home, takes them to the place for which they have always yearned. You saw it in their eyes. Then they have to choose whether to stay there or come back to reality. Of course, they always choose to remain. *Always*. But it's only a dream of home – a shadow. For there can be no journey's end without a real journey. Over time they fade away, become just shadows themselves.'

'Like those I saw in the reeds.'

The monkey nodded. 'They too came here like you, and ate. But the fruit dreams quickly become nightmares. And then . . .'

She broke off. Willum had stepped up on to the bows of the ship. A moment later he dived.

Willum swam across the lagoon to his friends. He staggered from the water, dropped to his knees and lifted Mr McCool's heavy head on to his lap.

'Wake up,' he whispered into the soft white ears. 'Please.' He peered into Mr McCool's eyes. The bear was still wandering over the ice, but the corners of the scene were no longer the frozen north. Willum swallowed. The colours of the fruit were beginning to form at the edges of Mr McCool's eyes.

When the monkey had worked her way round the shore, she found Willum cradling the polar bear's head. For a long time she peered at the strange sight.

'You are very special,' she murmured, her hand hovering gently over Willum's hair. 'And you can still escape. Look.'

Willum glanced up to see that the ship had drifted across the water and come to rest against a fallen tree at the mouth of the lagoon.

'Please go,' she begged.

'I can't. Don't you understand? They're my friends.'

The monkey hung her head. *'Friends?* I too came here like you, but not with *friends.'*

She looked so downcast that Willum felt a surge of pity. 'How *did* you come to be here?'

She sighed. 'You have met the one who brought me.'

'The organ grinder?'

'He was bound for the new world, and of course he took me. I was the best part of his act, the one people paid to see. When our ship first arrived, sucked here like yours, he gorged himself on the fruit with the other passengers, kicking me away though I too burned to eat. When my persistence angered him, he swung me round on the chain – that was always his favourite torture – but on this occasion he did it with such rage that the chain broke. And that was his last act. The next moment he was *asleep*.' The monkey almost smiled. 'His cruelty saved me. Seeing what the fruit had done to him, I did not eat. But even now, when he is just a shadow, I am still his prisoner.'

'How?'

She lifted the chain. 'With this round my neck, I cannot climb well. What kind of monkey can't climb? The wild ones fear me. They hear me coming and flee. All my life, I dreamt of being back in the jungle where I lived before a sailor captured me. As I danced and dodged the grinder's kicks, capered to his tunes, collected his coins, I longed to be here, with others of my kind. But although I am back I am still held captive.'

'But, little monkey,' Willum cried. 'I can set you free.' He scrambled over to where a stone lay. Picking it up, he began to hammer and saw at the metal collar. Trembling, the monkey watched the stone strike repeatedly. Sparks glinted and Willum's arm grew numb, but still the neck chain held. He began to fear some ghostly spell, when, with a dull snap, the collar fell off. The chain slid to the ground like a snake. With a screech of joy, the monkey sped away down the shore to where the river fed into the lagoon. Then, shooting up into one of the tallest trees, she was gone.

With a sad smile, Willum returned to his friends. The thought of a shadow-like Kansas forever wandering through the reeds was a knife to his heart. Again he tried to rouse them; again he failed. Slipping to the ground, leaning his back against Mr McCool, Willum buried his head in his hands. He had never felt this weary before.

The next thing he became aware of was a great seething in the reeds around him. He looked up in dismay, expecting to find a writhing knot of ghosts. Instead he saw monkeys. Over a hundred of them were assembling along the shore.

'I've explained it all to them,' the organ grinder's monkey cried. 'They will help.'

With much chattering and shrieking, the troupe lifted up the sleeping crew and carried them over to the ship. Two each took Kansas and Friend, a dozen bore Kingsley. The rest, after a loud debate, rolled the sleeping polar bear on to a lattice of strong-fibred vines, and bore him like a dead chief.

'I can set you back on the ocean,' Willum's monkey friend told him when the shipmates were all on-board. 'But no more than that. Perhaps I have just created a worse torture for you.'

'I'll run the risk,' said Willum, nodding firmly.

Using vines, the monkeys pulled the vessel back on to the river. Once in the current, the boat drifted swiftly downstream. The monkeys followed, swinging from tree to tree. Soon Willum saw that he was entering the sea. Willum's friend climbed the last tree and waved.

'Good luck,' she cried. 'And thank you.'

'Thank *you*,' Willum returned.

With a joyful screech, the monkey disappeared into the jungle with her troupe.

CHAPTER 11
. . . and Found?

The ship rolled in the ocean heave. Already the jungle coast was out of sight. The air grew steadily cooler – they were no longer in the doldrums.

On-board, only the vessel itself showed any sign of life. But the creaks and moans of timber and rigging, and the bows lifting and falling in the swell, merely highlighted the stillness of the dreaming crew. When darkness fell, Willum lit the lantern. Even the shadows cast by the lamp seemed to mock his loss as they flickered and danced over his motionless friends.

Lying amongst his shipmates, Willum thought of what they'd been through together. He recalled all their adventures, from the moment he'd first seen a polar bear panting in a concrete enclosure. And because it made him feel less lonely, he began to relate them aloud. He didn't forget the funny times either; he described each example of Kingsley's uppityness, told each of Kansas's jokes, relived every –

'No, no, no, you're getting it all wrong,' Kingsley suddenly burst out. Willum leapt to his feet. 'You're not describing me with enough panache,' the cat went on, sitting up and stretching.

Throwing his head back, Willum roared with laughter. He was still laughing when a loud caw rang out. The rook was flapping her wings. 'Well, I think you've got me accent perfectly, duckie, and it's not an easy one.'

'Friend!' Willum cried.

'Shoot, did we really do all those things, Androcles?'

'And Kansas!' Willum's heart jumped almost as much as the prairie dog, who had leapt into the boy's arms. Gratefully he buried his nose in the animal's soft fur.

'If anyone's going to tell our story, it had better be me,' Kingsley said. 'But first, two things require explanation: number one, we're in the ship; number two, we're at sea. When I ate the fruit we were . . .'

No one was listening. The others were gathered round the motionless body of Mr McCool.

'What you doing, big fella?' Kansas grinned, nuzzling his friend. 'You can't stay sleeping. The rest of us are up and about.' Mr McCool didn't even twitch. The grin disappeared as Kansas turned to Willum. 'Why won't he wake up?'

'Because he's lazy,' Kingsley said. 'I'll soon get him up.' He poked the bear, prodded him, caterwauled. Still Mr McCool did not wake.

Kansas's little snout quivered. 'I want Big Mac to wake up.'

Willum's joy curdled as he watched Kansas rub noses with Mr McCool, bark loudly and nip the bear's ears – all to no avail.

'Here, give us a go,' Friend said. She cawed, she crowed, she croaked, she hopped on his belly and flapped. Mr McCool did not move.

All night they tried to stir him. Day broke and the bear remained comatose.

'Is it just me,' Friend whispered to Kingsley, 'or is he going all thin and grey?

The cat nodded. 'As if he's fading away.'

In the growing light of dawn, Willum too could see that Mr McCool's white fur was becoming grey. *They fade away.* The little monkey's words echoed in the boy's head. *Become just shadows.*

Kingsley took Willum to one side. 'Now listen here, have you told me everything that happened at the lagoon? Don't keep anything back.'

Willum told Kingsley about the shadows in the reeds, and repeated what the monkey had said.

'Fade to a ghost?' Kingsley shook his head. 'No, no, no, one can't allow that. You'll have to wake him.'

'How?' Willum asked.

'Like you woke the rest of us. There I was, dreaming of a life of splendour and perfection, and then I heard *you* wittering on. I tried to ignore you, but humans have such *penetrating* voices.' Kingsley smiled warmly at Willum. 'What you did was make me realise that what is *real* is better than any dream. So I came back.'

'Why doesn't Mr McCool want to come back?'

Kingsley shook his head sadly. 'Don't forget, he's a zoo animal. Maybe he's roamed across the Arctic in his head for so long that he can't tell the difference between what's real and what's a dream. If you talk enough, perhaps he'll hear and decide to return.' Kingsley's voice softened. 'You can do it, Willum. If you, a two-legs, can make friends with a polar bear, then I'm sure you can do *anything*. Besides, I can't think of anything else.' He paused, and turned to the others. 'Right, you lot,' he called. 'Let's go down below. Willum needs to concentrate.'

'Please,' Kansas begged Willum as Kingsley shepherded them down through the hatch. 'Bring him back?'

Alone on deck, Willum crouched over the bear. Mr McCool lay utterly still in the halo of the lantern. Willum could no longer see anything through his eyes; they were almost totally sealed by the fruit colours. 'I've got to try to find you, Mr McCool,' the boy began. 'But I don't even know how to look. You're wandering somewhere. I know you didn't trust me, that you don't trust humans, two-legs, but we've become friends, haven't we?'

Willum began retelling their adventures once more, but his heart wasn't in it. Since their odyssey was ending like this, with Mr McCool fading in front of him, it no longer felt so grand. What else could he talk about? It didn't matter, just so long as he kept speaking.

'I'll never forget the day I first saw you,' he went on. 'You were lying in that enclosure and it seemed so wrong. I wanted to let you out.' Willum explained how his auntie had been waiting for him in the café. 'You'd like her. She was my mum's sister. I never really knew my mum.' The bear was growing increasingly shadowy – a pencil drawing being gradually erased. 'I know you lost yours too. Is it worse to lose your mum, or never to know her? I never knew my dad either. Are dads important to polar bears? They are to people, even when you've never had one. Sometimes I wonder if mine would have been proud of me. Sometimes I wonder if . . .' Willum buried his face in the bear's thinning flank. He couldn't watch his friend fading to a spectre.

How long had he been like that before he felt a light brush of breath on the back of his neck? Looking up, he saw that Mr McCool had woken. The purple mist was clearing; the bear was peering deeply into Willum's eyes.

'You've come back,' the boy whispered.

'Hello, son,' grinned Mr McCool.

*

They sailed north. Willum put on the warm clothes

Kingsley had tailored for him, to which the cat now added a scarf and a red woollen hat like his own. When night came, Kingsley set their course by the Bear's Nose. Their odyssey was underway again. The monkeys had filled their water barrels and left some food: wholesome breadfruit and nuts.

'What we need,' Mr McCool announced the next morning, 'is a good old knees-up.'

'A *what*?' Kingsley asked.

'You know, moggy – a shindig, a bash, a jolly, a jamboree, a bop, a jump, a good old let-your-hair-down. We used to have them in the zoo now and again. Remember, Kansas?'

'How could I forget, large lad. Shoot, let's have one now!'

Kingsley shook his head. 'Nice idea, rodent Rentokil. Pity it's impossible.'

'Why?' Mr McCool demanded. 'I fink it's just what we need.'

'My dear shagpile, one requires more than a few nuts for a party.'

'Better get your fishing rod out, then, moggy.'

'Can't be done.'

'Fought you could do anyfing!' Mr McCool grinned.

'Even I can't catch fish that aren't there,' the cat snapped. 'We need to find where the mackerel's running, or a shoal of herring. Actually, party aside, the cupboard truly is bare. No pun intended.'

Mr McCool's grin collapsed. 'Oh.'

'*Oh*, indeed, zoo boy. If we don't get some more supplies, we'll soon be going hungry, let alone partying.'

Lapsing into silence, the shipmates went about their tasks. Once again the threat of hunger was looming.

The next day, Willum was repairing the sail where some of the stitching had come undone, when he heard a faint tooting. It was as though someone was playing a strange, melancholy clarinet, high in the sky.

'Long necks!' Friend cried.

Willum looked up to see a huge flock of snow geese.

'What style,' Friend pronounced in admiration from the daybed she was sharing with Kingsley. 'What feather-and-beak music.' She beat her wings in imitation.

The gaggle's formation pattern constantly shifted as lead birds exchanged places, those resting at the back taking up their stint at the front. They flew effortlessly through the air like a living arrow.

'Well, what do you know,' Kansas laughed, dancing with excitement. 'They're showing us the way.'

The snow geese had formed a giant pointer.

'Follow that flock!' Friend cried.

Willum altered the sail. The ship changed direction and began to follow the geese. When it grew dark, they trailed the honking. All through the night they kept the goose-clarinet within hearing and come morning, the familiar and welcome cry was raised by all four of the shipmates at once: 'Land ahoy!'

It was a wide and beautifully desolate estuary, full of feeding geese and great flocks of waders. There was no sign of human habitation, a fact confirmed by Mr McCool's nose. Mooring up, the crew filled their water barrels from a stream, then gathered plentiful stores of seaweed, mussels, oysters and other seafood. When they had finished, they couldn't find Mr McCool.

'There he is,' said Willum, pointing over to where

the bear was paddling in a shallow river.

As the others watched, Mr McCool plunged a paw into the water and scooped something out. There was a flash of silver.

Kingsley chuckled. 'Well I never, his instinct's emerging. If I'm not very much mistaken, he's found a salmon run.' The great paw plunged again, scooping up another silvery flash. 'All good practice for when he reaches home. Funny, zoo animals don't usually *do* instinct.'

'He wasn't always a zoo animal,' Willum said. 'He was born wild.'

'Got snatched off the ice when he was a half-grown cub,' Kansas added. 'But not before his mum had taught him a thing or two.'

Friend nodded. 'Looks like those early lessons are paying off.'

'You know, that bear just might have what it takes to cut it in the wild after all.' Kingsley smiled.

A little later, fully loaded, the ship sailed from the estuary. 'As I was saying,' Mr McCool beamed. 'Time we had a good old knees-up. Moggy, Friend, get busy. You've a party to prepare.'

*

All afternoon delicious aromas wafted up from the galley. Kingsley had put a sign on the hatch: *Staff only, party-of-a-lifetime in creation*.

'What are you and Friend cooking, tabby?' Mr McCool growled at the closed hatch.

'Wait and see,' came the reply. 'Gluttony is *your* talent; stylish and tasteful occasions are more in *our* line.'

'It'll all be very tasty,' Friend cawed from behind the closed door.

'Can't I pop down and have a little smackerel of somefing? Me belly's farting like a walrus.'

'What part of *no* don't you understand?' Kingsley demanded.

With a happy sigh, Mr McCool lay on deck, breathing in the ever-growing party smells. Willum stood beside him at the ship's wheel.

'Where's the little fella? Mr McCool asked.

'He's still busy,' said Willum.

Since leaving the estuary, Kansas had been hidden away in a corner of the ship. From time to time the others could hear the busy sound of light gnawing.

'You finished whatever it is you're doing yet, little fella?' Mr McCool asked.

'Nearly,' replied Kansas.

'What you doing, little lad?'

'Surprise, big lad.'

At last everything was ready, and the crew came down into the hold. Clapping his paws together, Kansas bounced up and down deliriously. Fine cloths and soft furnishings from Kingsley's chest had transformed the hold. Bunting festooned the rafters; balloons had been blown and shaped exotically. Candle flames fluttered like butterflies. The table groaned with food and flavoured juices.

'Games first,' the cat snapped, rapping Mr McCool's paw as it stretched towards a bowl of moules marinière.

Cackling to himself, Mr McCool claw-scratched a circle on the wall's wooden panelling. Inside this circle, he outlined another, smaller ring, then sectioned them both with cake-slice divisions.

'That looks like a dartboard,' Willum said.

'Kansas,' Mr McCool announced in a voice that reverberated about the hold. 'Please step up to the capybara's tail.' The bear scored a line on the floor a few paces from the board.

'Me first, oh boy, oh boy!' Kansas laughed,

scampering up Mr McCool's arm.

'Old rules apply,' Mr McCool said, handing Kansas an object, which looked to Willum like a sharpened fish bone. 'Three flings apiece.'

Snout puckering with concentration, Kansas took his first throw. The little missile lodged on the edge of the board.

'A *zookeeper*,' the bear cried, handing Kansas another dart. This landed in the same place. 'Another *zookeeper*.'

Kansas's third dart lodged nearer the middle. 'Shot! *A full bucket of feed*. Friend, step up to the capybara's tail.'

Friend flapped on to the bear's arm. All three of her darts failed to hit the board.

'Fling again,' Mr McCool allowed.

This time she managed to score right on the edge of the board. 'One *zookeeper*!' the bear cried. The dart fell. 'One *dead zookeeper*,' he cackled. 'Tabby, step up to the capybara's tail.'

'And what a miserable tail it is,' said Kingsley, snatching the darts. His three tries flew wide of the mark. 'That board's too high,' he complained. His next trio of efforts didn't stick either. 'And it's too small.'

'Here, I'll show you how it's done,' said Mr McCool. He span his tusk then kissed it. One after the other, so quick that Willum could only see a blur, three darts flew to the dead centre of the board.

'Three *walrus noses*!' Kansas cheered.

'Who's the bear?' Mr McCool bellowed, beating his chest.

'*You're* the bear!' Kansas yipped. He climbed up his friend and high-fived him.

'Who dares challenge the bear?' Mr McCool demanded, strutting up and down so that his whole pelt bounced daintily.

'No one dares challenge the bear!' Kansas yikkered.

'If this is a taste of zoo behaviour, thank my lucky tail I've never done time there,' shivered Kingsley.

'Willum's fling,' Mr McCool chuckled. 'OK, boy, step up to the capybara's tail.'

Willum took the darts. Although they fitted the hand snugly, his three throws flew wide.

'You do it more like this,' Mr McCool explained. 'Close one eye slightly, and imagine you're stalking a seal on the ice. That's it.' Steadying Willum's hand, Mr McCool carefully lifted his wrist. 'Slow, slow . . . now!'

'A master-class in bone chucking – whatever next?' Kingsley grimaced.

The dart pronged inside the first circle. 'Shot!' Mr McCool cried.

'A *full bucket of feed*,' Kansas called. 'Say, you played this before, Androcles?'

Willum nodded. 'I had a dartboard on my bedroom door.'

'Straight up?' Mr McCool asked.

'It was a bit different,' Willum added.

'Seems we've more in common with humans than we thought,' Kansas grinned.

'Enough of this chavish pub pastime,' Kingsley complained. 'Haven't you got something more refined or intellectual to play?'

Chuckling excitedly, Kansas brought out a little box. Inside were two sets of small wooden figures – one black, the other light brown.

The bear gave a deep rumble of laughter. 'So *that's* what you've been up to all day, little fella.'

'Sure is,' Kansas grinned. 'Make the board, then, large lad.'

Mr McCool scratched out some marks on the floor. Willum peered down. It looked like a chessboard.

Kansas then placed the pieces on the board, the black and the light brown facing each other. Willum narrowed his eyes. They weren't *just* pieces. Were they carvings?

'Used to play this all the time, big fella,' Kansas grinned. 'Kind of miss it.'

'You start, little fella.'

Kansas lifted one of the black pieces and moved it two squares. 'Now your go, Big Mac.'

'Prairie dog to E4,' Mr McCool replied.

As Kansas moved one of the brown pieces, which were too small for Mr McCool to handle, it was caught in the candlelight.

'It looks just like Kansas!' Willum laughed.

'Who else?' Mr McCool chuckled.

Kansas took his own go then waited expectantly for the bear.

'Zebra to C3,' said Mr McCool.

A zebra figurine flashed in the light as Kansas lifted it. Willum whistled in disbelief. 'Are you playing chess?'

'You play *that* an' all, boy?' Mr McCool asked.

'Once or twice.' Willum smiled at the memory of all those games of electronic chess played in his bedroom. 'Our pieces are different.'

'Yeah? Your move, Kansas.'

Kansas lifted a giraffe diagonally across the board. 'We call that a bishop,' Willum explained. 'And instead of a rook you've got a tortoise.'

'I'm on a *human* chessboard?' Friend laughed.

'Your queens are lions,' Willum continued. 'And your king is,' he laughed, 'is a polar bear.'

'King Polar Bear, I like that,' Mr McCool chuckled. 'The little fella used to collect the wood from round the zoo and carve them wiv his teeth – just like what he's done today.'

'Hmm,' said Kingsley. 'They've got a certain primitive charm.'

'Made sets for the whole zoo,' the bear added.

It wasn't long before Kansas had been fatally cornered. 'You're Arctic skua meat,' Mr McCool announced.

Willum nodded. 'We say checkmate.'

Mr McCool beat Friend too. Starting brightly, Kingsley managed to capture a few of his opponent's prairie dogs and even a zebra, before the bear counter-attacked lethally.

'You're Arctic skua meat, moggy.'

'That's it,' Kansas shouted petulantly. 'I don't play with cheats.'

'Ain't cheating.'

'Course you are. How else could you have beaten me?' Kingsley demanded, flouncing off.

'King Polar Bear,' Mr McCool cackled.

'Willum's turn,' Kansas said. After a few moves, Willum snaffled one of Mr McCool's prairie dog pawns. 'Say, you've *definitely* played this before,' Kansas remarked, wide-eyed. 'Shoot, Big Mac, now you've got a proper opponent.'

The contest swung between bear and boy. Air humming with concentration, the whole crew hung on every move. Even Kingsley crept back to watch as Mr McCool leant over the board and directed Kansas to move his lion. A blunder. Willum closed in for the kill.

'Aha!' declared Kingsley. 'Who's Arctic skua meat now?'

Willum was one move from the end when a clawed paw swung over the board, sending the pieces rolling over the floor. 'Oh, sorry, stupid clumsy me,' Mr McCool said, his eyes avoiding Willum's.

'Of all the bad-losing, bad-breathed hearthrugs,'

Kingsley goaded. 'For years you've had everything your own way.'

Mr McCool glowered at his opponent. His head swayed threateningly. Then his stomach rumbled, and the whole crew burst into laughter. 'Sorry about that, Willum,' he said. 'Never lost before.'

'Little wonder with Rodent Robert the grain brain as your only opponent,' Kingsley mocked. 'Now come on, the banquet is ready!'

With a cheer, the crew set about the feast. It was the party to end all parties. At a single bite from one of Friend's specialities, huge oyster vol-au-vents, Willum felt the horror of the giants and sirens melt away. A mouthful of Kingsley's Quality Bilberry Cordial washed away the lingering taste of the lagoon fruit. Willum had just finished a third slice of chocolate cake when the music began.

'Welcome to the Kingsley Tail Dance Band,' the cat announced, springing on to a tea chest, paws chording a huge, spangled accordion. 'I may not be able to throw objects against a wall, wear bone bling or beat a cheating opponent, but just listen to this.'

A skirl of notes flew from the instrument and swooped round the hold like a swallow. Willum felt his foot tap, then bounce, as he was seized by the joy of the music. Along with the rest of his friends, he began to dance. They started sedately enough, but accelerated with the music into jigs and reels and rants. They pranced up and down the hold, ever faster until their steps made the candle flames dance too. Dizzying them with a series of lightning dosi-dos, the accordion then locked the shipmates into spinning couples, which spiralled out of control into laughing heaps. They picked themselves up and began to dance again. The night had only just begun.

'Can you play *Knees Up Mother White* on that squeeze box, Moggy?' Mr McCool asked.

'I don't do requests,' Kingsley replied loftily. 'I'm not some cheap music-hall turn.'

'You'll soon pick it up,' the bear advised. 'Very popular back in the zoo pens.' And with that, Mr McCool began to sing.

'A rather simplistic tune but catchy all the same,' Kingsley said when he had finished. 'But isn't it supposed to be *Mother Brown*?'

'Funnily enough, that ain't the polar bear version. Now the next verse.' Higher and higher Mr McCool kicked his legs, more and more riotously they sang, until the lamp swung on its rafter and the emptied bowls bounced on the table.

Coming to a final, rousing rendition, Kansas and Friend leapt on to Mr McCool's head, whilst Willum climbed on his back. 'Oh – Knees up, Mother White, Oh – Knees up, Mother White . . .'

After the dancing, Kingsley put his accordion to one side and performed his impressions. Rapturous applause greeted each one. Next, Kansas told his best jokes, followed by Friend, who recounted the tale of how Cousin Croak learnt to hover better than the kestrel. 'Now you, Willum,' Kansas called.

'I can't do impersonations or tell jokes,' Willum said. 'What should I do?'

'Tell our story again,' Kansas urged.

Friend flapped excitedly. 'Good idea!'

'I'll keep you right this time,' Kingsley put in.

Mr McCool nodded. 'Go on, boy. Tell it how it was.'

Chanting Willum's name, the others clapped and stamped and cheered until he stood up.

'And now,' the cat declared, 'the miraculous and inspiring adventures of Kingsley Tail.'

Willum smiled. 'This is the remarkable odyssey of Mr McCool and his extraordinary crew.'

When Willum had finished, Mr McCool took the spotlight.

'Another plebish ditty, hearthrug?' Kingsley asked.

'Nah,' said the bear, serious all of a sudden. 'A story.'

Kansas clapped his paws in delight. 'One of your mum's?' he asked. Mr McCool nodded. 'Is it about the *skittery-glittery* or the *little wanderers*?'

'One you ain't heard,' Mr McCool pronounced huskily. 'One *nobody's* heard. Cos I ain't never told it before. And it wants telling.' Mr McCool seemed to be peering deep within his memory. 'This is a story called "The Polar Bear Boy".'

'*Boy?*' Kingsley asked. 'It's about a two-legs?'

Mr McCool cleared his throat. 'Once a muvver bear fought wiv a walrus, and lost. When she never come back to the den, her cub went looking for her. He searched everywhere.' The bear nodded. 'Yeah, that's how it starts. Cub goes near a human village, didn't he? Now,' he continued, 'an old two-legs widow woman found the polar bear cub wandering where the villagers laid their fishing nets out to dry. *Where's your mother, little one?* she asked. The cub was terrified but, to his surprise, the woman didn't try to hurt him. It just so happened that, a year before, she'd lost her only son on a hunting trip, and the sight of the shivering little orphan touched her heart so much that she picked him up and took him home to her hut.'

'Shoot, that was kind,' Kansas whispered.

'And that's where he stayed,' Mr McCool told them. 'Summers came and summers went, and the orphan grew up as the widow's son. Neither of them was lonely no more. All the other children loved him. They called him Polar Bear Boy. They taught him how to fish and hunt, and he became the best fisherman, the best hunter.'

Warming to his story, Mr McCool had begun miming the actions, and his shadow flitted across the wooden panelling behind him like Polar Bear Boy stalking seals.

'But one day jealousy landed in the village like an Arctic skua and began pecking at the heart of some of the village elders wiv its sharp beak. Whispers started. *Polar Bear Boy's got too big, Polar Bear Boy's got too smart, Polar Bear Boy's* . . . In the end they got so jealous that they decided to do away with him.

Gathering one night, they hatched a plan to kill him.'

Kansas cowered under Friend's protecting wing as the storyteller's shadow seemed to form a group of plotters on the ceiling.

'Luckily, someone told the old woman. Fast as she could, she went to where her son was hunting. *They're going to kill you*, she cried. *Go and hide some place where only I'll be able to find you*. He hadn't expected this; he'd thought everyone loved him. Weeping bitterly, Polar Bear Boy ran.' McCool's silhouette lumbered across the wooden ceiling.

'The widow waited until the next day, then she went out to her son. Only she couldn't find him. Polar Bear Boy had gone right out on the ice and, during the night, the floe he was hiding on broke off and took him far out to sea. Calling his name, the widow searched all that day and all the next night, not knowing that he was swimming home. When Polar Bear Boy reached land, he found the widow half frozen, by the fishing nets. Now, he knew that if he didn't get her back to the warmth of her hut, she would die. But he also knew that if *he* went there they'd kill him. *Leave me here*, she whispered. *Save*

254

yourself, my lovely Polar Bear Boy. Picking her up, he carried her back to the village.'

Across the galley ceiling, the outline of Polar Bear Boy seemed to be carrying the body of an old woman.

'When the elders saw Polar Bear Boy's bravery, they was ashamed, and begged for forgiveness. Everybody else was overjoyed to welcome both the widow and her adopted son home again, and life settled back down to normal. The village became famous amongst both people and polar bears. Here was a place that was different from everywhere else. Here was a place where humans and bears lived together. Here was a place what showed the way it might be. Here was a place where a human and a bear could be a muvver and son, or even . . .' Mr McCool stared at Willum, who, peering back, felt his heart swell. 'Or even a farver and son.'

CHAPTER 12
The Meaning of Snow

Days of plain sailing followed the revels. The shipmates had become a real crew, and their barque, a princess of the salt sea. Willum felt that they weren't far away from the journey's end now.

One night during his watch, however, Willum realised that the Bear's Nose was not where it ought to be. He told Kingsley.

'That's because we're no longer sailing north,' the cat explained.

'Why not?'

'You'll see. Only don't tell ratboy.'

A day or so later, Kingsley raised the familiar cry: 'Land ahoy.'

'We got to the top already?' Kansas yelped, scrambling from the hold.

'It's not actually the Arctic,' Kingsley said evasively.

'Then where are we?' the prairie dog asked. Kingsley shrugged uneasily. Kansas turned to Willum. 'Where are we, Androcles?'

'You'd best ask Mr McCool,' Friend interrupted, avoiding the prairie dog's eye.

Kansas was skittering over to the bear when his nose caught a scent. Sitting up, he breathed in deeply. 'Earth,' he whispered. 'Mile upon mile of diggable earth.' He shivered with excitement. 'I can smell more earth than I thought could ever be. I can smell a prairie.'

Although Mr McCool tried to hide it, Willum thought he could see sorrow in the bear's smile when he said: 'We've brought you home, little fella.'

'Home?'

'To the prairies.'

'Kansas doesn't look exactly overjoyed to be here,' Friend remarked to Kingsley as they prepared to launch the skiff.

'Maybe he's just overcome,' Kingsley replied. 'He might be a prairie dog, but he's never actually smelt a prairie before.'

Friend shook her head. 'Looks distinctly *under*come, if you ask me. Maybe we should have warned him what we were doing.'

'And make the pain worse?' Kingsley said. 'No, no, better this way. Let the break be short and sharp.'

Feeling a surge of excitement at the land wind, Friend flapped her wings. Surprised by her returning strength, she flew right up, and with a croak headed for land.

Kingsley sighed to himself. 'Kansas isn't the only one who'll be leaving us soon. Pity. I'll miss her pastries, and her stories.' The cat watched the bird dwindle to a dot as she flew to the shore.

'Cheer up, little pal,' Mr McCool was saying to Kansas. 'This was always the plan.'

Kansas gulped. 'Kind of hoped you'd forgotten.'

That evening they lit a fire on the beach and spent their last night together as a full crew. Even Friend's stories couldn't cheer them up. Staring into the writhing flames of the driftwood fire, Willum told the tale of Prometheus, who stole fire from the gods. But the others were too preoccupied to listen. Parting loomed over them like the jaws of a trap.

'You awake, little fella?' Mr McCool whispered to Kansas in the small hours of the night.

'Can't seem to sleep, Big Mac.'

'Me neither.' The embers of the dying fire cast a feeble orange over the rest of the sleeping crew. 'Been finking, Kansas.'

'You have?'

'Instead of you just going off by yourself tomorrow, why don't we walk some of the way wiv you, help you find a nice burrow, get you settled in?'

To Mr McCool's surprise, the prairie dog shook his head. 'Better I just go by myself, make a clean break. No big deal, no drama.'

'You fink it's better that way?' Mr McCool tried to control his voice, but the thought of saying goodbye made him feel sick to his stomach.

'It's the *only* way,' Kansas shot back harshly.

Mr McCool looked up at the stars. All at once the glittering magnificence seemed daunting. 'Never thought I'd say this,' he murmured. 'But I almost wish we was back in zoo. Didn't realise saying goodbye would be so hard.'

In the darkness Mr McCool could not see Kansas's struggle to hide his emotion.

'You asked for freedom and you got it,' Kansas snapped. 'Now let me sleep, I've got a big day in the morning.'

Stung by his little friend's reply, Mr McCool turned on to his back. Shooting stars flared and died across the sky. Behind him the sea called him north; in front lay the land that would take his friend away forever. This wasn't what he had imagined when he had chosen freedom.

The crew woke at dawn to find that Kansas had gone. Mr McCool followed the trail of paw prints through the sand until he lost them on the land. Nose close to the ground, he set to follow his friend's scent. 'And where do you think you're going, hearthrug?' Kingsley demanded.

'Following him,' Mr McCool replied, his voice cracking.

Friend flapped her increasingly powerful wings. 'I'll find him.'

'You'll do nothing of the sort,' Kingsley said. 'Neither of you. It's been hard enough for Harry Hamster to make the break without you two tugging him back.' The cat gestured at the prairie.

'*This* is what he came for. To stop him now would be all wrong. Don't you agree, Willum?'

Willum couldn't answer. His throat thickened as he pictured the lonely prairie dog wandering across the endless grassland. Feeling something land on his shoulder, he looked up to see Friend perched there. Delicately, she preened his hair with the tip of her beak. 'You upset too, duckie?'

'He was my friend,' Willum replied.

The rook nodded gently. 'I know, but Kingsley's right. There comes a time when all living creatures must say goodbye. This is his.'

'He did it in style too,' Kingsley added. 'Went before we woke to save us the heartbreak. Mind you –' He looked over to where Mr McCool stood staring deep into the distance. 'Doesn't seem to have saved the hearthrug's heart.

'He thought the world of that little prairie dog,' said Friend.

'I wonder if the zoo-two still think this precious freedom of theirs is worth it,' Kingsley pondered. 'Come on, Friend, let's strike camp and get back to the boat. One down, four to go.'

As Kingsley and Friend packed up the skiff,

Willum went over to Mr McCool.

'He always trusted you,' Mr McCool said. 'Right from the start. He was like that.' The bear bowed his head. 'May he find his place to shine in the night sky.'

'I thought we only said that when someone had died,' Willum said.

Mr McCool gave a great sob of anguish. 'May he dance wiv the wind in the eternal grass.'

'May he find his burrow in the sky's earth,' Willum choked out.

One crewman less, the boat sailed north. Mr McCool no longer seemed interested in their destination. He lay motionless on the deck, just as he had done in his concrete pen. He didn't even seem to notice the temperatures plummeting with every passing day.

'We'll have to keep an eye on him,' Friend whispered to the others. 'That bear's not been himself since Kansas left. Gone off his food too.'

'Oh, he's still eating, all right,' Kingsley said. 'Does it at night. Things keep disappearing from my kitchen. We were supposed to serve one of your special raspberry tarts this morning, but *somebody* polished it off.'

'Comfort eating,' Friend nodded. 'He's missing Kansas. I tell you what, I'll make him a cheesecake.'

'Actually, I'm worried about the dolt too,' Kingsley said.

The nights were now so cold that Kingsley began lighting the stove. Mr McCool didn't argue; he slept outside.

'Time that bear pulled himself together,' Kingsley decided. 'We all miss Kansas, but moping around is the last thing Jeremy Gerbil would want. I've got a plan to foil tonight's midnight raid. Friend, you bake an extra-sized pavlova and I'll make one of my celebrated chocolate cateaux with buttercream filling. That should be enough bait, even for him.'

That night they left the food in tempting view on the kitchen surface, and instead of going into his newly made deluxe bunk, Kingsley hid in an empty tea chest. It wasn't long before the kitchen thief revealed himself with the sound of heavy breathing and loud chomping.

'Got you,' roared Kingsley, springing from the tea chest. But the culprit wasn't who he'd been expecting.

'Shoot, guess you caught me red pawed.' Kansas

stood in the middle of the cateaux, arms lifted in surrender, cheeks pouched full of buttercream.

'You deceitful, thieving, slippery, delightful rodent!' Kingsley burst.

Friend came fluttering wildly in. 'How did *you* get here, little bright eyes?'

Kansas giggled. 'Hid in the apple barrel. Came out to eat at night. Sorry about the food. I was going to show myself tonight anyway, figured we were far enough out for you not to take me back. Willum!' Seeing the boy, Kansas scurried up him.

'I thought you'd gone,' Willum cried in delight.

'How could I leave you all?' said Kansas, nose-to-nose with Willum.

Just then the hatch was thrown open and a bellow shook the kitchen utensils on their hooks in the rafters. 'Little fella!'

'Big Mac!'

'Looks like someone else has come back to life,' Kingsley grinned.

It was decided that they'd take Mr McCool home first and then drop Kansas somewhere suitable on the return journey.

'I don't mind cold,' said the rodent. 'Shoot, got kin who live in the ice. Do you think we could look up the Alaskan woodchucks when we get there, big fella? Hey, why don't I stay with them for a while? Have a nice long holiday. See you every day!'

It grew colder and colder. To keep the non-polar animals warm, Kingsley knitted suits from Mr McCool's spare fur. 'If anyone had told me I'd end up doing *this*,' he muttered, shivering as he combed the bear's pelt. But his grimace could not entirely hide his grin.

'Say,' Kansas began one morning as he and Mr McCool took the ship's wheel together. 'Haven't had a joke for a considerable time. What do you get if you cross a polar bear with a walrus?'

Mr McCool cackled. 'Dunno, what *do* you get if you cross a polar bear with a walrus?'

'A whole heap of trouble!'

They were still laughing when Kansas felt something cold land on his nose. Another icy kiss caressed his snout as he looked up. The air was dancing with great, white flakes.

'Big fella,' he whispered. 'Look.'

Mr McCool lifted his head and gasped. During the long years of captivity he'd only seen snow twice or thrice, and never anything like this. The flakes fluttered down from the sky like feathers; already they were beginning to lie on the ship. Yelping in delight, Mr McCool began to caper like a cub.

Down in the hold, Willum heard the happy shouts and came up to find his friends frolicking in the snow.

Pirouetting like a sumo ballerina, Mr McCool flopped on his belly and slid over to Willum. *'Forgive and forget,'* he whispered solemnly.

'What do you mean?' Willum asked, smiling at Kansas, who was burrowing through the deepening fall.

'Old polar bear greeting, innit, Willum. We say it when meeting during the first proper snow of the year.'

'Why?'

'It's what snow does. Covers the ugly and makes it beautiful. Hides mistakes. Forgives and forgets.' Mr McCool dropped his head. 'I'm sorry,' he whispered.

'What for?'

'For doubting, and blaming you. For finking all two-legs are bad. For forgetting the story of the Polar Bear Boy, for believing that humans and bears always have to be at loggerheads.'

'I forgive and forget,' Willum said.

Mr McCool tried to say something else, but nothing came out. Instead, he leant right over and touched noses with Willum. A snowflake landed at the point of impact. In sheer delight, Mr McCool opened his mouth wide. Willum did the same. They were savouring the delicious taste of melting flakes when a huge snowball burst between them.

'Come on, landlubbers,' Kingsley cried. 'Kingsley Tail, the fastest snowball thrower on the seven seas, challenges you to a grand snowball fight.'

CHAPTER 13
You Ain't Lived . . .

The day after the snowball fight, the temperatures rose again. Their snow-sculpted figures started to melt. There'd been one for each of them: rook, prairie dog, cat, boy and bear. Now only the largest remained, the bear, a gradually shrinking figurehead at the ship's prow.

'What's going on?' Kingsley demanded from behind the wheel. 'Should be colder than this. I thought we'd have encountered our first iceberg by now.'

A little later a loud caw rose from the top of the mast where Friend was perching. 'Land ahoy!'

The crew gathered at the bow and saw that they had sailed into a wide bay. 'This is it,' Kingsley declared. 'The Arctic at last.' He narrowed his eyes to

peer at the flat coast. 'Can't see any bergs or glaciers.'
He turned to the others with a quizzical look. 'I can
see flowers. Odd.'

'I didn't think there'd be flowers in the Arctic,'
Friend said.

'Mile upon mile of flowers,' Kinglsey confirmed.
'They're rather fetching actually.'

Mr McCool's head craned to one side as he tried to
make sense of the fragrance filling his nostrils.

Kingsley continued: 'Yellow, white, pink. A blaze
of colour. But not an icicle in view.'

'Flowers?' Mr McCool blurted out, bewildered. 'In
the name of the eternal ice, what's going on?'

'Come summer there's flowers every ways you look,'
Kansas declared, a dreamy look in his eyes. *'Me and
me sister used to lie in the cotton grass, and watch the bees
all day. Then we'd listen to the curlew singing.'* Kansas
grinned. 'Don't you remember your own words, big
fella? This must be the Arctic summer. The tundra's
brief blaze of life.'

'Rather absent-minded of you to forget that,
hearth-rug,' Kingsley remarked. 'The way you go on
about it, one would think it was the eighth wonder
of the world. But wait a minute. Aha! I *can* see an

iceberg. Look! If I'm not very much mistaken, isn't that the sun reflecting off it?'

The crew peered at a bright glimmer on the sea.

Mr McCool swallowed. 'An iceberg?' he rasped excitedly.

The closer the ship sailed to the iceberg, the more dazzling its reflection grew until it was a riot of brightest white.

'That's not an iceberg,' Friend laughed. 'It's a flock. The winking of many white wings.' She sighed. 'If only they were black.'

Mr McCool gaped at the birds. 'What are they?'

'You ain't lived till you've seen the Arctic terns playing in the air,' Kansas whispered, quoting his friend again.

'Little wanderers,' Mr McCool murmured.

'I don't think much of the hearthrug's long-term memory,' Kingsley remarked to Friend. 'First he forgets the unforgettable sights of the tundra summer, then he can't recognise a flock of Arctic terns.'

'Well, he's home now,' said Friend.

The terns were feeding just offshore. A splash doused the vessel. Mr McCool had jumped in.

Invigorated by the sea's cold embrace, he swam strongly. A family of seals slipped from a rocky outcrop and, bobbing in the water, warily watched him pass. Reaching the stony shore, Mr McCool hauled himself up on hind legs. With water streaming from his lithe and now brilliantly white flanks, he scented the air. The summer tundra stretched for as far as the nose could see.

With a yelp of excitement, he waded through a yellow meadow of Arctic poppies, then shambled across an acre of cotton grass nodding in the breeze. Even the rocks were in bloom, their golden lichens shining like miniature suns. Bees buzzed; dragonflies flashed. Mr McCool splooshed through shallow pools and padded over blankets of reindeer moss. He was at a thicket of low-growing bushes, cramming his mouth with berries, when a wading bird with a long, curved beak rose up from the grass. Flying overhead, it scattered a lingering song.

Mr McCool nodded to himself in wonder. 'Curlew,' he rasped.

He roamed on, skirting puffin nesting chambers, careful not to stand on the little birds whose beaks seemed to have been dipped in a rainbow. A cloud of small, white finches broke over him as a large brown bird planed across the tundra.

'Arctic skua!' he laughed.

At last he reached the tern colony. Lumbering into its midst, he looked up to where the agile sea swallows swooped and lifted, beaks flashing silver with the little fish they were carrying to their hungry nestlings. It was as though he had staggered into a bird blizzard.

'I'm back,' he shouted to the *little wanderers* who, every year, fly the length of the planet twice. 'Been wandering almost as far as you.'

Geese honking, shore birds crying, Mr McCool dandered on across the blossoming plain: the return of the native.

All at once he stopped, hooked by a scent both familiar and yet utterly strange. He craned his head, trying to solve the mystery. Then he realised. It was the scent of another polar bear. There it stood in the distance. A female. Something began singing in his heart.

Breath suddenly ragged, he tottered forward. Without understanding why, he lay down and rolled over extravagantly. He heard himself bellow. The female heard too and playfully scurried away. Head spinning with unfathomable excitement, Mr McCool galloped after her. He had never seen anything so beautiful as the female's loping stride, nor scented a perfume as wonderful as her musk. The years of zoo incarceration fell from his shoulders. This was who he was meant to be: a wild animal roaming through a beautiful wilderness.

They chased each other playfully through bushes and flowers, through pools and the shallows of the sea. They raced across beaches and vast stretches of cotton grass. They tottered on hind legs and sprinted on all fours. They swam across inlets, and fished in fast-flowing waters.

Lost in their games, the two polar bears were taken by surprise when suddenly they felt the ground shake beneath their paws. They looked around. The tundra was exploding into agitated life. As though fleeing some catastrophe, geese and waders rose in shocked flocks; herds of caribou stampeded, hares, foxes and musk oxen charged headlong. Mr McCool looked up. Overhead, a helicopter was thumping towards them.

Mr McCool stood his ground. Head swaying, paws flailing, he defied the metal tornado.

Nearer and nearer the aircraft wailed. It came so

close that his fur ruffled in the downdraught; so close that he could see the man leaning out; so close that he could see the gun the man was pointing.

Instinctively, Mr McCool spread himself in protection of the female, but she'd already gone. A shot rang out. Something hit him like the cuff from a giant paw, and he fell. He tried to get up, but the claws of the cuffing paw held him down. Darkness was settling over him. Again and again the gun fired.

As the two polar bears had been playing, Kansas was sitting on the gunwale, staring out across the bay. 'The big fella's been gone too long,' he said to Willum, who was standing at the wheel. 'Should be back by now.' The prairie dog began to yikker and bark.

'What's all the commotion?' Kingsley demanded, poking his head up through the hatch.

'Time to send out a search party for Big Mac,' Kansas urged. 'Anything could have happened to him. He might be lying hurt somewhere or maybe he's –'

'Relax,' Kingsley interrupted. 'What could go wrong? The hearthrug's back on his home patch.'

'Shoot, he hasn't been up here since he was a half-grown cub.'

Kingsley shook his head; his voice became gentle. 'Now listen here, Kansas, he's going to be leaving for good soon. You'll have to get used to it.'

'Already?' Kansas whispered.

Willum picked up the prairie dog. He hadn't noticed the grey whiskers on his snout before. As he cradled Kansas in his arms, sharing his warmth, he heard what sounded like the beating of a hundred drums – dum-dum-dum-dum. He looked over the bay to see rotor blades slicing the air. A helicopter was beating its way over the tundra. At that moment, the first shot rang out.

'That's more than any farmer's gun,' cried Friend.

'Quick!' Kingsley shouted. 'The hearthrug's in trouble. We've got to go to him. Tack the mainsail.'

The sounds of gunfire and the helicopter were coming from behind a high, rocky peninsula. Kansas and Willum hurriedly altered the sail and the ship headed in that direction. What they saw as the boat rounded the wall of rocks made Friend hide her head under a wing and Kingsley's ears flatten. Willum gaped. After the beauty of the tundra, the scene before him seemed unbelievable.

Full of holes and crevasses, the shore resembled nothing so much as the face of the moon or the no-man's land of a battlefield. Gouged into, hacked at, tortured – the beach was a gaping wound. And it wasn't just the land. From here, they could see a metal island perched in the middle of the bay like a steel crab. Two towers rose from it like pincers. A writhing pipe chimney flashed bright flames.

'What is it?' Kingsley asked.

Willum could not bring himself to reply. Who could have guessed that in the midst of all this beauty they would find an oil field?

When he was a cub, Mr McCool's mother had taught him that when polar bears die a flock of snow geese carry them up to the great tundra of the sky. Was that why he could hear the snow geese now, and feel the thrum of their wings as close as the beating of his own heart?

Opening an eye, he saw the world far, far below. On the shore, his friends were gathered round a large white body. Yes, the snow geese *were* bearing him away from this world, taking him on his final journey to the stars. He smiled. It had all been worth it; the years in prison had been healed by the miracle of freedom.

'You'll have to have your liberty without me, little fella,' he called to Kansas. 'Make sure you live it large.'

Higher and higher he was borne until he felt as though he must be near the stars. Someone was calling his name. Again and again, it called. Was it his mother?

Despite the sadness at leaving his friends, Mr McCool's heart surged with joy. He hadn't seen his mother for so long. 'I'm coming!' he yelped. Feeling the geese set him down, the bear looked up. A distant light shone from above. Like a cub leaving the den for the first time, he scurried towards it. 'I'm coming,' he cried. Already he could see the constellations: the Raven, the Wolf, the Arctic Fox, the Human. The *human*? It was a human that had slaughtered his mother; it was a human who had just shot him. Humans were all bad. No, Willum had taught him that not *all* humans were bad. They too had their place in the stars.

Mr McCool let out a cry. How close the

constellations were. Near enough to touch. Funny, they seemed smaller now that he was so close – the Wolf was cat-sized, the Arctic Fox like a rodent, the Raven was more of a rook, and the Human was just a boy.

With a shuddering gasp, Mr McCool opened his eyes. What he had taken to be stars were his friends. He hadn't died after all.

CHAPTER 14
Saying Goodbye

Hidden by a screen of feeding terns, the ship pulled out to sea. The flock continued to camouflage them until they were well out of view of the helicopter and oil rig.

'Thanks, *little wanderers*,' Kansas shouted.

The bullet had only stunned Mr McCool, grazing through his thick pelt. A centimetre closer and he would still be lying on the tundra shore. Yet, after a day's rest, he was up and about.

They sailed further north. Mr McCool sat at the prow, nose scanning the northern horizon. A change had come over him. The wildness that Willum had noticed in his eyes that first day at the zoo was growing. He spoke less, growled and rumbled more.

It grew bitterly cold; the first ice was expected any

day. The others gathered round the stove. 'He'll be going any day now,' Kingsley said. 'I just hope *everyone's* ready for it.' He glanced at Kansas, who was sleeping on Willum's lap beside the stove. Despite his proximity to the heat, the prairie dog was shivering. A change had come over Kansas too. Stiff-limbed and aching, it seemed that all at once he had become old.

Kingsley sighed. 'Yes, it's all coming to an end.' He turned to Friend. 'What about you?'

'They said they'd seen it,' Friend whispered. '*The little wanderers*. Said they knew where my flock was. Said they'd lead me to it.'

'Why haven't you gone, then?' asked Kingsley with a sad smile.

Friend's soft croak was almost like a dove's coo. 'We have to get Mr McCool home first.'

With a weary stretch and a yawn, Kansas woke at last. 'Say, what's that?' he asked, pointing at the porthole. Strange patterns had formed on the glass. 'They're beautiful,' Kansas wheezed as he struggled off Willum's lap and limped over. He tried to reach up to the glass, but couldn't. Willum lifted him so that his forepaws could rest on the patterns.

'Cold,' Kansas said, wincing.

'Ice flowers,' Kingsley explained. 'The glass is so cold our breath condenses on it and freezes. We're nearly there. We *must* reach the ice soon.'

'Nearly there,' Kansas murmured. 'Nearly home.'

'Now, don't worry yourself,' Kingsley said gently. 'I'll go and make you some cocoa.'

Later that day, the hush which had been steadily creeping over the ship was shattered by Mr McCool's sudden roar of wonder.

Pulling their furs on, the crew hurried on deck. Willum tucked up the sleeping Kansas by the stove, and followed. The cold sucked his breath away and crackled at his eyes. He joined the others as a huge finny tail lifted from the sea.

'It's a blue whale!' he gasped.

'Thar she blows, and other assorted clichés,' Kingsley said as the huge whale surfaced, a parabola of water gushing from her back.

'They're the largest mammals in the world,' Willum declared in amazement. 'Look, there are more.'

One after another, the blue whales rose to view. The pod was five, ten, fifteen strong, each member far bigger then their ship, except for the calf who swam in their midst.

'What a flock. So big, but so gentle,' Friend said, flapping her wings in admiration.

'*Whales loom, ice soon.*' Mr McCool murmured the old polar bear saying to himself.

The pod had just passed, silent, graceful, when the crew saw something floating into view.

It was an iceberg.

'Well I never,' Kingsley cried. 'It's –'

'It's Mr McCool!' Friend cried.

The iceberg, floating alone, did indeed seem to have the shape of a polar bear. They watched in awe as the natural sculpture sailed silently by.

The ship soon encountered larger bergs. Sailing under a great white arch, the crew found themselves in a cathedral of ice. Glittering pillars rose to a vaulted roof far, far above. The boat negotiated huge altars of frost, frozen towers and shining, white steeples before leaving through another archway to a narrow canyon of open water.

'Well, Kansas,' Mr McCool said. 'What do you fink?'

Kansas wasn't there.

'Where's the little fella?' Mr McCool demanded.

The rest of the crew exchanged looks.

'He's not feeling very well,' Kingsley explained.

'Hey?'

'We didn't want to worry you, but ever since the tundra he's not been so chipper,' Friend said.

'He's just taking a nap,' Willum added.

'Nah, he won't want to miss this,' said Mr McCool, rushing down below.

At the sight of his friend dozing in the armchair, Mr McCool's great joy faded. Kansas's sleep was laboured; his breath fluttered like a butterfly with a broken wing.

'We've made it,' Mr McCool stammered when Kansas opened his eyes weakly. 'The Great White. We're on top of the world.'

'Shoot, we did it. Knew we would,' said Kansas, in a peculiar wheezing voice. He fell back asleep. When he woke again, he found himself held snugly in Mr McCool's warm pelt.

'Hey, Big Mac.'

'Hey, little fella.'

They both tried to grin.

Night was falling at the portholes as the ship sailed

past searing crevasses and towering pinnacles of ice.

'What you doing here, large lad?' Kansas breathed; it was harder and harder for him to speak. 'Should have gone by now. You're home.'

Mr McCool's voice was choked. 'Ain't going. We'll turn round. Take *you* home.'

'What about the *skittery-glittery*, the glaciers, the –'

'All that can wait. We're going to settle you first.'

A sad smile played over the little grey snout. 'Too late.'

'Got it all worked out, Kansas, you see –'

'There's not going to be any home, big fella. Not for me.'

Mr McCool hung his head. 'I knew it. It's my fault. Should never have let you come up here to the cold.'

Kansas reached out and rested a light paw on his friend's nose. 'Not that. Just run out of time. Told you before we set off I was too old for all this.'

'Behave yourself, little fella.' Mr McCool forced himself to laugh. 'It was only yesterday that you was born. I remember the first time I saw you, a tiny ragamuffin of a prairie dog kit; the only one bold enough to come into me pen.'

The bear broke off at the look in Kansas's eyes.

'Many prairie moons have fattened and thinned since then, large lad. I've reached the end; all my tunnels have been dug.'

A tear burnt its way down Mr McCool's face.

'Don't be sad, old friend,' Kansas said. 'I've lived a lot in my short time. Remember: *one day of freedom . . .*'

'*Is worth more than a lifetime behind bars,*' Mr McCool finished.

The prairie dog reached up to wipe away Mr McCool's tear. 'Say, can't you hear the icebergs calling you?'

For a long time they both listened to the strange creaking sound filling the hold: icebergs rubbing against each other.

'How can I leave you, Kansas?'

'You've got to. The time has come.'

A coughing fit engulfed Kansas. When he spoke again, Mr McCool had to bend right down to hear. 'Do it for me; do it for all of us, Big Mac. Show that even the biggest dreams can come true.' With a great grimace of effort, Kansas placed his paw in one of the bear's. A sob throbbed from Mr McCool's throat, but the prairie dog's face was lit with joy. A brilliant skirl of light played over his features. 'Look,' he managed to whisper. 'Look!'

Columns of colour were pouring in through the porthole, bathing the galley in brilliance. The aurora borealis was dancing over the North Pole.

Mr McCool gaped in awe at the *skittery-glittery*. 'We've done it, little fella. We've got here.' When he looked down at Kansas to share his delight, his friend's eyes were closed, never to open again. A smile was on his snout.

'May he feel the eternal prairie wind through his fur,' Mr McCool murmured.

'And dig a thousand holes,' Friend added.

'May he dance amongst the prairie flowers,' whispered Kingsley.

Willum's voice wobbled: 'And know the peace of the spring rain on rich earth.'

So it was that they said goodbye to Kansas.

The next day they reached the permanent ice shelf. The ship could sail no further north.

Willum found Mr McCool at the prow. 'Are you ready?' he asked.

Mr McCool nodded heavily.

'I'll miss you,' Willum said. With a heavy heart, he waited for his friend to jump down on to the ice and disappear into his rightful element. But Mr McCool showed no sign of going.

'Ain't no use,' he suddenly gasped. 'Can't do it.'

'You'll soon remember what to do.' Willum encouraged him. 'It'll come back to you.'

'What will?' the bear asked in a strange, small voice.

'Who you are – you were born here.'

The wildness in Mr McCool's eyes flickered and faded. A haunted look took its place. 'That's the problem, Willum. You see, I ain't who you fink I am.'

'What do you mean?'

'Never been here before, have I.'

Willum shook his head in bewilderment. 'But you were snatched as a cub. They took you from the ice.'

Mr McCool sighed. 'Never happened. Born in the zoo, me. I ain't never seen no tundra summer, no *skittery-glittery*, no icebergs. Put it this way, before our voyage, far as I knew, the *little wanderers* might have been pigeons.'

Willum's mind span. He could hardly believe what

he was hearing. 'I don't understand; you know all about it.'

'Everyfing I know about the white world, I got from me mum. Grew up listening to her talking about the old country, didn't I. But them stories and songs were the nearest I ever got to freedom. It was *her* what was born in the snows, not me. *She* was the real McCoy: a wildling.' Mr McCool sank to the deck, head on paws. 'As time went on,' he continued. 'I told the stories as if they'd happened to me, even came to believe me own lies. But she was the one what got snatched as a half-grown; she was the one born wiv the white winds in her heart.' A sad murmur escaped the huge jaws. 'Oh, Mum, what did they do to you? You died young, went before your time, wasted away, melted like an icicle. The wild ones always do, Willum. It's the bars, innit. They break their heart. Only the old lags like me last. When all you've known is a piece of concrete, somehow you just put up with it. But now it's truth time. I'm no more wild than you. You can take the bear out of the zoo, but not the zoo out of the bear. I'm only glad Kansas never lived to find out. Even the tusk was hers. I was never able to earn my own.'